# The

# Time Traveller's Quest

## Dave Young

Dave Young was born in Edinburgh, Scotland in 1947. He has owned and managed many small businesses, dealing with people from all spectrums of life. He is a graduate of Visual Arts Cert 3 and Cert 4.

He came to Australia with wife and three children in 1984.

He has written a lot of short stories, many set in his home town of Edinburgh, both historical and modern day.

Although this is the first work to be published, he has other work, which may be published at a later date.

Dave is currently working on an 'underbelly' character set in the sixties and seventies. His character rises from a life of petty crime, in the rough and tumble of Edinburgh's night scenes, to one of notoriety.

# Prologue

In 2015, as the CERN Proton Accelerator was propelling matter at 99.9% of the speed of light, it was noticed that miniscule wormholes had appeared. Thus the speculated hypothesis of time travel was becoming closer to a reality.

Noted Physicists such as Stephen Hawking were now conceding that time travel was possible. Scientists in the Accelerator laboratory were trying to form one wormhole from the multiple miniature ones - in the same way as mercury when divided into tiny balls will join together into one fragile mass.

One scientist from Edinburgh, Scotland, Ian Sinclair is the first to master the technique.

To the surprise of all, whilst the wormhole mass is being kept stable a ghostly figure appears holding some kind of box. The figure disappears again without completely materialising.

Meanwhile, back in 1999, posts were appearing on the Time Traveller's Institute message board. They claimed to be from a time traveller from the year 2036. His mission slowly unfolds in the form of Internet message posts, but then disappear just as abruptly as they had started.

Why was this time traveller here?

What is his mission?

# Chapter 1

He was blinded by the high beam of oncoming headlights as his car cornered the narrow lane. He was off with his wife and daughter for a weekend of relaxation, before taking up his Swiss appointment.

The impact of the four-wheel drive on his modest saloon car resulted in the death of his wife and daughter. Only time would heal the grief and feeling of guilt for being the sole family survivor.

He went to Switzerland earlier than proposed, to immerse himself in his work to keep his mind off his recent mental torment. Ian Sinclair was no ordinary Physicist He had excelled at Edinburgh University and had PhDs in Neuron Science and Atomic Particle Structure. His talent was natural and he had always been eager to learn more in these fields, hence the invitation to assist with the large team at the CERN Particle Collider in Switzerland. This was a unique opportunity to express his talent. As usual, he learnt at a tremendous pace, and within a week he was comfortable with the team of new associates. Although Ian was a Professor and Doctor of Science he only used these titles when publishing a paper. To his new team he was simply, Ian.

He was drawn to one of the team, Lucy Stanford. Not in a romantic way, but as a meeting of minds. They discussed how even after only a few years their Doctorate degrees were already outdated and both strove to keep up-to-date with any advancement in their fields.

Ian was so immersed in his work that he was not eating properly and would work up to twenty-two hours nonstop, catching a couple of hours sleep over his desk. The team were concerned for his welfare. Whilst he was making major inroads in particle collision, he was in danger of 'burning out'.

Lucy was chosen by the team to gently slow him down before he actually broke down.

"Hi Ian, how are you this morning?" she asked looking at the dark rings around his eyes.

"Yes. Yes, fine," he replied in a distracted manor.

"Have you looked in the mirror recently?" she asked jokingly.

"What?" Ian responded as if the words had not penetrated. He was in a world of his own.

"Listen, Ian! The team are worried about you. You're not eating properly and hardly getting any sleep. Jim Stewart suggested that I talk to you, but I don't want you to get the wrong idea. Could we go for a meal tonight? I need some advice on my project. I'm sure you'll have the answer. It's slowing down the rest of my work and I need to resolve it.

Ian looked up, a different expression on his face, now. The distant look was replaced with one of confusion.

"What did Jim say exactly?"

"Just what I said. Don't worry, it is only out of concern that he spoke to me, and I DO need help."

Ian thought for a moment. He realised he could not remember the date and was unsure how long he had been working like this.

"Perhaps I do need a break," he conceded. "Yeah, we'll go out tonight. I'll let you make the arrangements, book a table that sort of thing." I haven't been out since Ruth and Helen died, he thought to himself. A brief feeling of guilt swept over him as he thought of his wife and daughter - something that he had avoided confronting by immersing himself in his work.

"Meet me at the entrance, maybe seven o'clock," he suggested.

"Yeah. Great!" Lucy smiled in reply.

The facility had halls of residence. They were a cross between University-style and four-star hotel accommodation. There was a canteen termed 'a restaurant' which was centred in the hub. Ian realised now that he needed to get out of the place for a while. Lucy was waiting for him at the entrance.

Security was tight - they had to sign out using hand print technology. They also had their own personal swipe cards to access different parts of the facility. The CERN Collider was twenty-seven kilometres long buried under the surface. The complex was huge and employed over seven thousand personnel in different but related disciplines, as well as cleaning and catering staff. Computer technicians had their own building. The collider took major power when working at full capacity. So much so, that power had to be taken from the adjacent French grid to support it. Computer skills in many fields were needed, all with different security levels.

"I've booked a table at a little Chinese restaurant," Lucy told him, hoping for a positive response.

"I love Chinese food, you chose well."

Finding a taxi wasn't a problem. With seven thousand staff, taxis were coming and going twenty-four hours every day. Ian hadn't explored his surroundings, and had not been paying attention when Jim Stewart picked him up at the airport. It was a twenty-minute taxi ride to the restaurant and only now did he begin to take an interest in his surroundings.

Lucy paid the cab driver, ignoring Ian's attempts to reimburse her.

"I hope you can help me resolve what I've found, it's baffling me." Ian noticed that she had brought her iPad with her.

They went into the warmth and chose a corner table. Neither of them was much for small talk, so Ian got straight to the point.

"What did you want to discuss? But first, let's order, then we won't be distracted."

They both quickly chose dishes, which they decided to share. Ian declined any wine, but Lucy chose a glass of house white. She grimaced at the first sip. Obviously a cheap Chardeaux, he thought.

Lucy turned on her iPad, opened a folder then a sub file, and handed it to Ian. It was all is algebraic equations, which he had no problem reading.

"This can't be right. Looks like you've found miniscule nano wormholes," he laughed.

"I've checked it three times. Jim says I must have something wrong, but if I have, I can't find it."

The food arrived and Lucy insisted on putting the iPad down until they had eaten. Ian could not contain his curiosity. Had she blundered into some quantum leap in the study of particle matter? His mind was spinning, but Lucy held firm and insisted on eating before discussing it any further.

"This is the first time I've been out since my wife and daughter died," he said.

Lucy was aware of his tragic loss but was unsure how to answer him.

"I can't imagine such a loss," she said with genuine caring. "They say time is a great healer, but those who say aren't going through your experience." She chose her words carefully not using 'grief' or 'accident'.

"I know I need to move on, but if I immerse myself in my work it seems to lighten the load so to speak." He looked directly at Lucy and said, "Please don't feel uncomfortable mentioning it as everybody else does. I'd rather face it than bury my head in the sand. Thank you for caring." He had a slight smile, the first for a long time.

"Now, let me look at those equations again!"

She opened her iPad and let him study the work she had done. His mind was quick. He scanned the work time and again.

Ian was incredulous. "You've found miniscule black holes at the precise point when matter collides. If we could assemble these together, we could form a wormhole. A passage to a time portal! I can't wait till we verify this tomorrow."

They got a cab back and went their separate ways.

The next day he scrutinised her work and found no fault. He phoned Jim and asked him to come as soon as possible.

"I thought she must be mistaken," said Jim "But it's your field of experience."

"Do you realise the potential here?" Ian asked.

"Possibility of time travel?" Jim queried, open-mouthed.

"Spot on!"

# Chapter 2

Ian had very little sleep that night. He could hardly contain his excitement. His mind raced on. He knew that he had to slow down and look at the discovery from outside the box, from a lateral perspective.

He was also aware that if news got out there would be an international fight for the rights. The whole CERN operation was multi-funded, so each country involved would want to get their hands on it. The finding had to be contained. It was still only a theory. They hadn't managed to find a way to proceed - to join the wormholes together. There was a lot of work to be done. And they had to do it! It was a field he and Lucy specialised in.

Ian was at his desk early. There were coffee machines on every floor, and he was on his second cup when Lucy came in.

"See if Jim Stewart is in yet." Ian was taking the lead and Lucy was happy to follow.

"Jim's on line two," she said.

Ian summoned her into his office and motioned to close the door. Pressing the flashing light on two, he spoke in a direct manor at a fast pace. He outlined his concerns and said that there were probably a hundred more he hadn't thought of.

"Can you come to my office straight away?" he asked. "Please don't mentioned this to anyone - we need to do a brainstorm on this and keep the lid tightly shut."

Within minutes Jim was sitting in Ian's office. Although Jim was technically the senior member of the team, Ian had the specialist expertise, which was needed in this case.

Once Jim was seated Ian didn't waste time. He reiterated his words to Lucy including the necessity to keep the finding between the three of them.

"To be honest, I was so excited about your findings that I hadn't thought through all the issues and implications. We don't want World War III breaking out over this." Jim was joking, but Ian wasn't smiling.

"If you think it through to its obvious conclusion that would be a very real possibility." Ian was very serious and he wanted the other two to fully understand the implications.

He went on. "I think that we have the expertise to gather enough of these wormholes together to form a mass, but keeping it stable is another matter. It could be as fragile as a ball of mercury." He was looking thoughtful and the other two listened intently.

"Jim, I need an assistant with expertise - someone we can trust." They were both looking at Lucy. "Down the track we will need the IT boys but on a strictly need-to-know basis."

"Look," said Jim. "I suggest that you take full control with Lucy. Just keep me in the loop. I'll make sure that you get all the help you need." Jim was still looking excited, straining to contain himself as he left the room.

"Where do we start?" Lucy was keen to play her role.

"We need to talk it through step by step. I'll show you how I think we can stabilise these wormholes that you've found." Ian wasn't going to waste any time.

He drew out equation after equation without stopping on a large paper pad. To the trained eye it was a work of art and Lucy was right up there with him. They worked nonstop until early evening, neither realising the time slipping away.

" I think you're very close," Lucy said, "but what about this last line here?"

"That's the problem we will have to resolve." Ian's mind was racing again trying to grasp the answer. It was close! He knew it, but it just kept escaping him.

"Let's stop and pick things up tomorrow," Lucy suggested. Reluctantly Ian agreed.

"Why have you used a paper pad?" Lucy asked innocently.

"Well, call me paranoid if you like, but I don't believe that our computer systems are as well protected as we're led to believe. The Chinese will be working 24/7 trying to hack into our mainframe. They now have some of the best hackers in the world. Long ago instead of punishing young hackers, they were nourished and encouraged to challenge the Western World's systems. Governments and multinational global companies all have secrets to hide."

She was embarrassed by her naivety. "No, you're not paranoid, just cautious," she conceded.

Now Lucy paused. She wanted to broach the subject of time travel and bring up something she found on an Internet blog site when she was a student. She hesitated and then plucked up the courage.

"Perhaps your going to think me gullible, but when I was a student in the late nineties, there was a blog from a time traveller. He had a huge following at the time. I think it was 1999 when it started and then he just disappeared in early 2000."

"Lucy, given what we have found, we have to consider all possibilities no matter how stupid you think they may be. Please tell me - I promise not to laugh."

"Can we go down to the restaurant and discuss it there. I'll bring my laptop to do research."

"OK – we'll discuss it first then if I think it has merit we'll do a search. But we need to make sure that we don't raise anyone's curiosity about what we're up to."

Perhaps he is a bit paranoid, Lucy thought, but she bowed to his life experience and wisdom.

They walked in silence to the lift — not for any security purpose, but both deep in thought.

At the twenty-four hour buffet they helped themselves, then chose a corner seat.

Lucy spoke between mouthfuls.

"Back in 1999 — I think it was October or November — a blog site was picking up posts from a John Titor. He said he had come from the future, 2036 I think. He said he had gone back to 1975. My roommate at the time was fascinated and kept talking about it. To be honest, at the time I thought time travel belonged to H.G. Wells and subsequent sci-fi writers, but now here we are facing a distinct possibility." She put her fork down and looked at him for some kind of reaction.

"Well, up until yesterday, I probably would have laughed it off, or at least put it in the too hard basket. But we now have to examine every possibility. We must open our minds to anything that may help with our work no matter how silly it sounds. But I think that we should keep such ideas to ourselves for now. That way Jim won't feel he's being made a fool of. I don't think that he is ready for any other earth shattering news just yet."

"OK," she smiled. "Do you want to check the Internet for any sign of this John Titor character?"

"What website was he posting on?" Ian asked.

"I think it was The Time Traveller's Forum," she replied, opening her laptop.

On the website there were no posts from anyone called John Titor. But the entries only went back twelve months. Lucy tried a blog history search for John Titor, but still no luck.

"Well over fifteen years," said Ian. "Try just John Titor." Lucy obliged.

"Oh, look at this!" she said. "There are quite a few references here. Even got a memorial site!" she laughed. "Perhaps it was all just nonsense - somebody with a vivid imagination or even worse, depending how you look at it — someone selling John Titor merchandise. I now remember my roommate sent away for a cloth badge with a peculiar insignia. She sewed it to her jacket."

"Listen! Trawl through whatever links and threads you find and let me have a summary tomorrow." Lucy nodded eagerly; even knowing she would be up half the night.

"You know what strikes me," Ian said, as they rose to leave. Lucy looked at him expectantly.

"January 2000! The Y2K Bug! I'm wondering! Would you come back to such an event, if only to watch from the sidelines? Remember people were waiting for Doomsday. Planes flew virtually empty as the midnight hour came to pass. Also, I'm thinking — what's important about 1975?" He looked at her as she made a mental note of what to look for.

"See you in the morning," he said, as he walked off to the lifts.

She felt like a student again after the lecturer had handed out assignments. But this was much, much more exciting and important. I'm a member of the team that is about to make earth-shattering history, she thought. She would not get much sleep that night.

# Chapter 3

Lucy had been up until four o'clock researching as Ian had asked. With only a couple of hours sleep, she thought she would be first into the office, just before seven o'clock. But Ian was already sitting in front of his computer, a cup of coffee at his side. He looked up and gave a brief smile as she sat in front of him.

"OK," he said looking directly at her offering his full attention, "I guess you've made some interesting discoveries. Doesn't look like you've had much sleep." Lucy realised it was obviously showing, but her enthusiasm had conquered any lack of sleep.

"Well, I followed a lot of links and threads, a lot of it Internet blog nonsense, but I've got a summary of interesting bits here." She produced a hand written record of the summary of her searching. "Ian, I have to ask, do you think that you or we can stabilise a mass, and if so, is time travel really possible?"

"Well, we believe that it is hypothetically possible to travel forward, but as to going back in time, the consensus is that the 'laws of nature' would make it impossible — the old scenario of what if you go back in time and kill your grandfather. Would you then cease to exist?" He looked at her. She was obviously absorbing every word, wrapping her mind around a subject that she would have laughed off even a few weeks ago. "But with our new discovery, or should I say what you have found, we should ask what the possibilities are. We have to open our minds. We must not let what we were taught in the past as being fact, now determine how we proceed with our work. What did you find last night?"

Lucy refrained from saying it was after four when she went to bed, instead referring to the notes that she was holding. She quickly starting reading through, but was interrupted before she finished.

"So, what to do think of this John Titor character?" he asked scanning her face for a genuine reply.

"Well," she hesitated, "I think that it makes sense in a lot of ways, even though he doesn't mention the Y2K Bug. If I was time travelling, I would certainly stop off to see how people were reacting. Remember some people went to the mountains. Others had food and water supplies and firearms ready to protect their families. There was a definite fear in the wider community and it had a lot of news coverage."

"Yes, I remember. I flew from The States to London with Ruth and Helen who was just a baby at the time. We were the only three onboard. The captain announced it was past midnight and all was well. All computers were working normally. Cheapest flight I've ever had. Airlines were drastically discounting flight prices, as people were too scared to fly. Anyway, please continue!" He nodded to her with encouragement.

"Well, his story makes sense in a lot of ways, but his predictions have not come to pass. One strange one was Bovine spongiform encephalopathy or Mad Cow Disease. It had already come and gone by 1999. I think the all clear was given in 1994. But he spoke of it as a prediction. Also he predicted a civil war in the United States, which hasn't come to pass. He predicted it would culminate in five different States being established."

"Anything else?" Ian asked. He was waiting for something definitive; something he could think was plausible.

"Well, he did mention his reason for returning to 1975 and what his mission was." Ian suddenly sat up to attention. Would she now reveal the factor he was waiting for? "He said he had gone back for an IBM5100 computer. I Googled it and it turns out that it was the first portable computer. It could be connected to the IBM 'home host' computer by a dedicated landline. The 'home' computer would have been four times the size of your office. The 5100 model's cost was about US$11,000, I don't know what that is in today's money, but a lot I guess."

"Double it I reckon," said Ian. "So what would he need an IBM5100 for?"

"He said it was to fix a bug that was about to happen in all of their computing systems in 2036, but didn't specify what."

"OK," said Ian. "Anything else?" He looked quizzically at her, his mind pondering the enigma of an old IBM computer and what possible relevance it could have twenty years into the future.

"If it's any help, he said he was working for the military and it was a specialized and dangerous mission. He was to go back in time to a specific date, 1975, and then return to 2036. I don't know if stopping off for the Y2K Bug on his return journey was his own idea. All a bit confusing?" she questioned.

"Not really," he replied. "Did you find out anything else about this IBM5100?"

"I did a full search. Then searched IBM in general. Nothing sprung out at me. But I don't know what I'm looking for." She had a puzzled expression on her face.

"Let's stop a minute," Ian said. "I want to be clear about what we've covered to date. We've found wormholes that we are close to stabilising —it should be what is close to dark matter or a viable 'black hole'. If we manage to do that, then — CAN we time travel? If so, what are the difficulties to overcome? How do we set a date to go to, and how do we ensure that we return to the exact time we departed from? There are a lot of questions to answer."

"Perhaps if we could stabilize enough matter we could then examine it in detail, and then consider the problems that you've mentioned," Lucy suggested. She was confused and not convinced that her discovery would make a viable wormhole to travel in.

Ian smiled. He showed her the now familiar note pad. She scanned the algebraic equations she had made, but he had taken it to the next step.

"Let's try, and see what happens," he smiled. "Tell Jim to book us time on the Collider and tell him to come with us while we try out my theory."

* * *

The next day at 3pm they had the Collider to themselves. It was so big that there were always maintenance staff working somewhere on the twenty-seven kilometre circuit.

"I've authorized a 'need to know' time booked for now. So there's virtually no one around to watch," Jim informed them. "I must admit I'm intrigued."

Ian started up the accelerator. A bit like an MRI machine, it took a few minutes to gain maximum speed. It was propelling atoms at 99.99% the speed of light, seven thousand times faster than the time displayed on his wristwatch. It was basically in a different space-time continuum.

"People have difficulty getting their head around this time warp," Jim said. "Imagine how we will have to explain what we've done and found."

"Now!" Ian interrupted him. He was frantically typing commands into the Collider's computer. Suddenly there was a strange grinding sound and they saw that the cameras were picking up something.

"Hope you're recording this," Jim suggested.

Ian ignored him. He was intent on what he was doing — totally engrossed and oblivious to his surrounds, apart from the screen to which he was glued, frantically typing in minor adjustment commands.

Gradually, a ghostly figure appeared carrying what looked like a box, but the image dematerialized just as quickly as it formed.

"What the hell happened?" asked Jim. Lucy was looking incredulous. She had a good idea what happened, but was finding it hard to believe.

"We stabilized some matter for a few seconds," said Ian. "Needs working on," he said in a matter of fact tone. Obviously he believed that he had worked out how to stabilize a large cluster of dark mass, and he was disappointed it had dispersed and disappeared so quickly.

"Play back the camera images," Jim said. There were many laid out in the tunnel. Some were extremely high-speed. Ian picked out the best high-speed shot to look at, and rolled forward to the ghostly figure.

"Incredible!" said Jim. He did not have the benefit of Ian and Lucy's research and the John Titor character.

# Chapter 4

Lucy was a bit stunned by what had happened, but she thought that the ghostly figure was possibly John Titor with his IBM5100 computer. However, she realised she must wait until they were alone to discuss it with Ian.

Jim left them at the controls of the now shut down Collider.

Lucy was eager to discuss the events just witnessed, but she knew that security was an issue.

"Fancy going out for a meal again?" she asked him. He was still distracted, obviously trying to work out how to finetune his work.

"Yes, I certainly would. Seven o'clock at the entrance, I'll let you work out the arrangements again," he was still deep in thought and his response was as if part of him was on some type of autopilot.

It was four o'clock, so Lucy had a few hours to kill before going out. She once again returned to her laptop to search for something that might help. She typed in 'time travel' and was faced with many pages. She waded through the first twenty. There were several sites of interest. She opened one called 'The Laws of Time Travel', which had been written by a noted Physicist, Mark Brady. She read it over a couple of times. It concurred with what Ian had said —that the established view was that you could not go back in time, or if you could, it could only be to when the first Time Machine had been built. She pondered his speculative work. But now that she had witnessed a possible contradiction to this she was confused and made a mental note to take it up with Ian.

Ian was again a few minutes late as Lucy waited by the entrance. "Where to?" he asked making no apology for keeping her waiting. She could see that he was still deep in thought.

"An Italian restaurant tonight," she replied. He nodded showing no indication of whether he was happy with her choice.

Again they got a taxi straight away and Lucy gave the driver the restaurant location. They sat in silence. Lucy was keen to discuss her findings, and Ian was distracted by the only partial success of the experiment. Soon they arrived and this time Ian was quick to pay the driver before Lucy had a chance.

It was a charming little restaurant, fitted out in an Italian style. They made their choices from the menu, and this time Ian agreed to try some wine. They ordered what appeared to be a respectable red. When they had been served their entrees and started their first glass of wine Lucy could resist no longer. "Do you think that was John Titor that we saw this afternoon?"

"I think that it is a good possibility. You didn't say anything to Jim, did you?" He was no longer distracted and had become more focused.

"No, of course not. I thought you felt you could trust me." She felt a bit hurt.

"Sorry! I do trust you. It's just that we have to keep this under wraps until we know what we're dealing with. I think that I've worked out the adjustments needed to stabilise the mass." She looked expectantly at him waiting for more. He took another sip of wine and allowed the waiter to bring their main course, before continuing.

As soon as they were alone again he talked nonstop. He had evidently worked out how to resolve the initial problems and was keen to try again.

"If we can fully stabilise the mass, we have to figure out a few things. How do we build a machine? How do we programme it? We obviously will need onboard computers. How will they react in a different space-time continuum? If we power the whole thing with batteries, will there be enough power? We can't use solar energy that's for sure." He smiled as he could see Lucy begin to fathom the complexities of it all.

She had ordered pizza but was now playing with it rather than eating. Her mind was totally overwhelmed. She now had to forget a lot of what she had learned about nuclear and particle science. Everything that she had taken as 'gospel' was being re-written in front of her eyes. She had never been adventurous as a student, in fact quite the opposite. She had forgone a lot of the party scene at uni to buckle under and achieve all of her degrees. But now, almost ten years later, she was being confronted with undeniable evidence of the possibility of time travel and wormholes. However, she had a high respect for Ian and his capabilities. Although about ten years his junior, they had an excellent working relationship, which was getting stronger as the weeks went by. She looked up to him as a father figure and mentor in this specialised field. But now! Now she was trying to suppress feelings, which were almost like an adolescent crush. She blushed at the thought trying to put it out of her mind. Back at uni her roommate had had an affair with her tutor that had ended in disaster. She had to focus and put any romantic feelings out of her mind. Also, she knew that Ian was probably still mourning the death of his family, even though it was over a year ago now. How could she even feel this way? She must clear her mind and concentrate on the work in hand.

Ian, on the other hand, realised he was relying more and more on Lucy as an assistant both in the lab and in a general secretary's role. Half the time he just assumed that she would do this or that without thinking of her considerable qualifications. He knew she was happy to assist because it wasn't every day you had the opportunity to be part of something as earth shattering as the work they were currently processing and shaping.

Ian was still distracted until he suddenly looked directly at her.

"I think I've found the basis for a time travel machine." It was as if this thought had just burst out on its own. "I'm going to draw up a rough drawing of the specifications. We need Jim in on this now. Can you tee up a meeting for the three of us tomorrow sometime? I'll draw something up tonight." He was starting to look excited at the plan that had formed in his mind.

Lucy was impatient to find out what he had formulated, but realised he was not ready to disclose it yet. How on earth was he going to overcome the problems and issues they had discussed earlier? He was certainly a man on a mission. Also he was suddenly looking tired as if the recent mental gymnastics had drained him. She would just have to wait until tomorrow. Could he really have devised a viable Time Machine? She would have to be patient.

# Chapter 5

When Lucy got into work just after seven o'clock, Ian was at his desk. He had obviously been up most of the night, now running on adrenaline.

"Get a hold of Jim as soon as possible. In fact, go and leave an urgent message at his office then come and join me. We can go through my draft plan. I would appreciate your feedback."

She felt a bit flattered. He was asking for her opinion on such advanced and yet-to-be-tested matters. She did as he had asked and spoke to Jim's PA, leaving the message as Ian had directed. She then got a coffee from the machine.

"OK! I've been in suspense all night. Can we have a look at your design?"

Ian looked pleased with himself as he brought the drawing up on screen. It was in three parts — a plan, an elevation, and one at 45 degrees to give a 3D effect. It was a typical technical drawing specification. She looked in awe. "Did you do all this last night?" she asked.

"Yes," he replied, trying to contain his excitement.

He pointed to the 3D effect drawing, stretching it out to fill the screen. She could see that it was neatly hand drawn and had obviously been scanned to his computer, avoiding putting it into the facility's IT system.

She could see circular disc-shaped objects sandwiching five main components. He pointed to the disc shapes.

"These are electro magnets. You can see the three main ones on each disc. They will rotate in opposite directions, a bit like an antigravity machine. This will also stabilise the machine, like gyroscopes used in aircraft. As you can see it's a bit like a sandwich. Just below the top disc is an electron injection manifold to alter mass and gravity of micro singularities…."

"Hold on!" she exclaimed. "In plain English please! What are mono micro singularities when they're at home?" She was an accomplished physicist but this was getting beyond her comprehension. Ian had just assumed that she would be keeping up with him.

"They are the small mass portals that we thought were black holes, but in fact they were tiny wormholes. We need to keep the mass that we have stabilised, and we need to keep it in a manageable form if we are to proceed."

"OK, what's that underneath?" She was pointing to the next part of his 'sandwich'. She was starting to wish it were just a sandwich, as they were now at or beyond the cutting edge of science.

He smiled at her. "It's a cooling and ventilating x-ray system."

"So, what's that for?" she asked, wishing she was a bit brighter. She had never felt as inadequate as this before. She voiced her feelings.

"Look!" he said. "You've done exceptionally well up to, and including now. I can assure you Jim will have no idea of how this drawing will work, but unlike you, he will not admit it. Relax, you're doing fine. You're very quick on the uptake."

Lucy blushed as the feeling of attraction passed over her again. Focus, focus, she thought, trying to only think of the complex machine jumping out of the screen at her.

"And next?" she asked.

"Gravity sensors!"

"At least I know what they are." She was pleased that there was something she could immediately recognise. "They're the sensors used in smart phones and tablets. They measure the vector components of gravity when the device is at rest or moving slowly."

Ian smiled at her. "Spot on," he said. "And these?"

"They're the machine's main clocks measuring time in nanoseconds." She felt pleased with herself at again recognising another part of the machine. "And here," she pointed, "just above the bottom disc, is the main computer unit, or should I say units. It looks like three."

"Well done!" he said. "You've grasped the main concept."

Lucy felt like she was back at school and being top of the class. She appreciated the praise after stumbling through the first part of the drawing.

"The discs top and bottom, are they like the antigravity machine that Nicola Tesla patented in the late 1920s?" she asked. She had a vague memory of a fellow student, a conspiracy theorist, who told her that the oil companies had bought the patent and suppressed it. They of course did not want people travelling for free —the whole oil industry would collapse.

"Yes. It was in fact 1928, and one of his last patents. I was at university with Michael Fleming. His parents had come to the UK just before WWII. His father worked in the patents office and was disturbed that Nicola had no business sense. Because of this, he secretly copied many of his patents, hoping to find a good use for them. In fact, many of Nicola's inventions, like x-ray, fluorescent light, and a lot more were stolen by wealthy industrialists. When Michael's father passed away, Michael inherited them. I was fascinated with the antigravity machine idea and tried to memorize the general principle. So the discs that you see top and bottom are a modification of his theory."

"Wow!" Lucy was impressed. "You've certainly got what seems like a viable plan for a machine," she went on.

Thinking for a moment, she asked, "Just one thing, how will you set the time? Say you go into the future, how will you be able to set a time to go back to?"

"We need one of the wizards from the computer department. Someone who can be discreet." He looked at her, a slight smile on his lips. He was teasing her.

"OK, you've obviously got some crazy plan in mind!" She waited for the answer, no matter how insane it might be. The last couple of weeks had been mind boggling, so not much would surprise her now.

"Stonehenge!"

"You are joking!" This beggars belief, she thought.

"It's four thousand, six hundred years old. When it was built, during the Summer and Winter solstice the sun would rise precisely between the heel stone and capstone. Just like gun sights! Of course after all this time they no longer align. It's perfectly obvious to the naked eye. We can go to Stonehenge at, say, the Summer solstice next month and survey the difference between now and four thousand six hundred years ago. Then using the facility's computer, compute to nanoseconds where we stand in time comparatively."

She looked at him. It wasn't that crazy after all.

"Say the traveler wanted to come back to his departure date, the onboard computers would have to, give or take a week, compute a precise time to come back to."

"Exactly!"

They were interrupted as Jim charged into Ian's office. He was never one to announce himself.

"Not interrupting anything?" he asked. He was the type who was always telling risqué jokes and finding sexual connotations where none existed. Ian privately thought it probably made up for his inefficacy in bed, it usually did.

"No. We've been waiting for you," Ian said curtly. "The mass we stabilized is a wormhole, a portal if you like. It's certainly not a black hole." He now pointed to the drawing on screen and went over it step by step, just as he had with Lucy. He could tell that Jim had misgivings. He said nothing, but Ian could sense his lack of excitement. This was because of his failure to understand the finer points of the machine and it created his inability to move with their new discovery. Jim was still unable to shake his long held beliefs taught to him over many years.

Although Ian would need Jim's approval, he realized he must wait a couple of days to bring up the Stonehenge idea.

Not wanting to embarrass himself, Jim left congratulating Ian on his progress. After all, he thought. I'll get the credit for all of this when it succeeds. If it fails I'll make sure Ian takes the fall. This was the typical hierarchy thinking at most academic facilities.

When they were both alone together Lucy turned to Ian. "What do you think is the significance of the IBM machine?"

"Don't know!"

"Well! I've found something very interesting in my Internet travels. On the first of January 2038, computers will start to run backwards. Like a Y2K Bug, but even worse. Apparently all computers were programmed by IBM from the first of January 1970. Even though they display the time and Gregorian calendar for our convenience, they are in fact running on a thirty-two-bit cycle, and of course, the IBM boffins never considered the future significance. To them, 2038 was too far into the future and would be of no consequence to them. All computers since then run on this cycle, which is very complex, so no one has bothered to change it. So! Maybe John Titor needs an IBM to re-set their computers to save an oncoming catastrophe."

It was Ian's turn to say, "Wow!"

# Chapter 6

Lucy and Ian strolled along the corridor to Jim's office. Lucy had made the appointment, but had not been specific about its reasons. Although Jim was department head, he never seemed to do anything of note. He would always mumble that he was working on this or that, but it was easier for him to say he was supervising one of the many different projects being conducted by his ever-growing team. Lucy didn't particularly warm to him, but realised she had to respect his position. Ian, however, was not as tolerant, and Jim knew it. For this reason Jim gave their lab a wide berth, leaving them to only send him weekly reports, which he no doubt attached his name to before they were sent up the ladder.

"Come along in," said Jim trying to signify his higher-ranked position, to which Ian was oblivious. Lucy, however, watched with amusement as Jim squirmed with the knowledge of Ian's qualifications and extensive expertise.

"So, what's on the agenda?" Jim asked looking directly at Ian.

"Well, it's complex," said Ian. "Remember the draft Time Travel Machine I showed you the other day?"

"Yes, yes." Jim looked uncomfortable, unsure if he was going to be asked an awkward question.

"We need to ascertain a space time continuum. Or time specific to the space we occupy at this moment."

"Yes," said Jim, still hesitantly.

"Well, I've thought of a way to resolve it. But I need to fly to Bristol then drive to Stonehenge to formulate a precise method. We will need to use the facility's supercomputer when we come back. So we need someone who can work with us in a confidential manner." It was Ian's turn to look at Jim directly. He was looking a bit lost.

"I can't understand for the life of me what an old stone monument has to do with any of our work here." Jim was wondering if Ian had been working too hard and lost the plot a bit.

"Stonehenge was built four thousand six hundred years ago. It may have had other uses, but one we are sure of is the alignment of the Summer and Winter solstice between the capstones and heel stone. It no longer aligns because our planet has moved in relation to the sun over the millennium. We can survey the Summer solstice next month on the twenty-first and using sensitive surveying instruments, measure the difference between where the sun is rising now, and where it was then. We can then compare it to where it would have risen, inline with the heel and capstones thousands of years ago. Then we run the results through the supercomputer and the difference of alignment will give us a 'time specific' point of any time we need."

Jim looked flustered. He was in charge of a department at the cutting edge of nuclear science and here was one of his subordinates rambling on about some godforsaken druid monument. He was struggling to justify the concept, even though it was starting to make some sort of sense.

"We'll need experienced surveyors, permission to access the sight all those sorts of things." Jim was trying to avoid being involved in what some would see as some type of fantasy.

"My cousin in Shrewsbury is an architect and he will put a very reliable and reputable surveyor at our disposal. I've spoken to him and he's happy to meet us at Bristol airport and arrange all the logistics. We have flights provisionally booked, but just need your OK."

"Well I suppose," said Jim. "But if there is a department inquiry about expenses I'll be putting you in the firing line."

"I wouldn't expect anything else," said Ian.

Jim wasn't quite sure how to take his reply. He then took refuge in mumbling that he had another urgent meeting to attend to and left them standing in his office.

Ian smiled at Lucy.

"I don't have flights provisionally booked," a note of panic was evident in her voice.

"Well you heard the man, book them now." His smile was endearing when he had accomplished something, and again she had to fight off her crush on him, which now led to a tingling down her spine.

Lucy did as directed and made all of the arrangements. She booked the flights. Spoke to Ian's cousin Andrew to confirm their airport pick up and booked accommodation close to Stonehenge. It was a bed and breakfast in a seventeenth century house. It was in Church Street in Amesbury, in the old centre of Salisbury. It was called the Arms Lodge. The rooms looked good on line, but she had been caught out before. On impulse she dialled the phone number on screen.

"Arms Lodge, how can I help you?" The young female voice sounded bright and friendly.

"Hi, my name's Lucy. I'm Ian Sinclair's PA and I've just booked two rooms in that name. The thing is, last time I booked accommodation it was nothing like the photos online," she lied. "You sound honest. Will my boss be happy with what you offer?" She was trying to sound the efficient secretary, but not sure if she was pulling it off.

"The rooms are bright and clean and renovated two years ago. There's a small bar downstairs and we offer a full English breakfast." There was a slight Scottish lilt to the accent.

"OK. I'll take your word for it. Mr Sinclair can blame you if he has any issues."

"He won't," was the confident reply.

"Oh, I've just thought. I may need three rooms." Lucy was thinking of Jim's cousin.

"I'll keep three," the girl replied, "but with the Summer solstice coming up we tend to be full. I'd be obliged if you could confirm the third room as soon as possible. My name's Heather by the way."

"OK, thanks for that Heather. I'll confirm within twenty four hours." Lucy looked again at the magnificent old building. How romantic she thought. I'll bet the original family who owned it never dreamed it would become a B and B. She was aware that death duties and the high cost of maintenance were forcing once wealthy families to adapt or lose everything apart from their title. She was glad she had phoned. Heather sounded very efficient, yet warm and welcoming at the same time. She then phoned Ian's cousin who confirmed it would be great if he could stay with them for the couple of nights. She immediately phoned Heather back and confirmed the three rooms.

Lucy found Ian and confirmed all of the arrangements.

"Great," he said, as if it was something she did every day.

"The girl at the hotel said they would be booked out for the Summer solstice. Will that be a problem for us with so many people there?"

"No! The whole area is fenced off and the Druids and sun worshipers will have to do whatever they do at the other side of the fence line. We do have a permit, which Andrew has arranged, so it won't be a problem."

The next few days were taken up with finetuning and stabilising the wormholes that they had found. Jim was copping flak from other departments who used the Collider, but managed to stand his ground.

The following Monday, while working with the Collider Ian managed to actually create a wormhole and stabilise it. It was strange looking through it. It was a tunnel, then it wasn't; it was a golden yellow, then it had all the colours of the rainbow, and then it went to ultra violet. At this point Ian managed to fix the hole. It was only he and Lucy at the Collider controls. Jim was nowhere to be found. Ian was still concerned that they may create a black hole and the gravity would then be so great that it would literally swallow them up. This was a hypotheses widely held in some quarters.

Lucy had been looking in awe at the almost hallucinogenic and hypnotic display. The ultraviolet hue was bright and the hole was shimmering.

Suddenly the ghostly figure appeared again. But this time it began to materialise. A figure in some type of uniform was walking towards them carrying a box. Lucy was feeling totally freaked out. She had once taken a tab of acid at uni, but that was nothing compared with this experience. This time she couldn't calm herself with the knowledge she was on lysergic acid. This was real! Ian, however, was calm at his console. He kept one eye on the controls and the other on the figure now almost solid. Ian reached his hand out, but it passed through the figure.

"Are you John Titor?" he asked of the now steady figure. There was no reply. Ian again put his hand up to the figure. This time there was resistance. The figure was becoming solid. A few moments later it began to speak.

"May I put this down, it's heavy?" He referred to the box that he was carrying. By now Ian too was trying to keep calm.

"Yes. Of course! Let me take it," said Ian.

"No!" the figure said sternly. "It needs to stay beside me. Perhaps you have a chair or something I can rest it on."

Ian couldn't help but notice the distinctive IBM logo on the box. Lucy was frozen to the spot, but Ian grabbed a chair. The figure rested the IBM box down.

Again Ian asked, "Are you John Titor?"

"Yes, I am, but I probably shouldn't be here. I'm on my way back to 2036. We have anticipated a major computer problem coming on the first of January 2038 and we need an IBM computer to fix it. This is one of the first portable computers built that could be plugged into the IBM mainframe which was used to programme a date to run on."

Lucy had been right thought Ian.

"The thirty-two-bit cycle will start to run backwards and we need to re-programme them from the original hardware," Titor went on.

This is unreal, Lucy thought. Ian was having the same thoughts. What do we do with this character now he's here? Ian cleared his mind.

"John, I think that we are on the verge of time travel, I wonder if you can help."

"The laws of time travel are very specific," said John. "Just like the laws of nature. You can ask questions, but some I literally can't answer."

Ian's mind scrambled to think of relevant and specific questions to ask. Was he on the right track? He was about to find out.

# Chapter 7

Lucy was transfixed, not quite believing what she was seeing. Ian however. was eager to communicate with the figure, outlined in the purple hue of the wormhole. He noticed that John had not let go of the IBM computer, always ensuring part of his body was with it at all times.

"Could I ask why you cannot let go of that old portable computer?" he asked, and then rebuked himself. There must be much more significant questions, and who knew how long the apparition would last.

"If I lose touch with it, it will probably go back to 1975 where it came from. I'm part of the Special Services Force and went to a great deal of trouble back in 1975 to get it. There's probably a warrant out for someone fitting my description. Whether I stole it or not depends which time continuum you come from. But the last thing I want is to go back there again. These IBM5100 units are few and far between; very few were manufactured."

Ian noticed that his uniform had the same logo Lucy had showed him from the John Titor memorial web site. "I guess I should be asking the most pertinent questions I can think of," said Ian, "but your appearance has been a bit of a shock to us. You spoke of the laws of time travel and equated them to the laws of nature. Can you expand on that for us?"

Lucy had recovered enough to start recording the conversation on her smart phone. Probably need to replay it a few times she thought. She remained silent allowing Ian to take charge of the proceedings.

"Well, I can only tell you what you already know, or hypothesised. Regarding the latter, I can only tell you if you are correct or not. I can't leave this portal as my machine is programmed to voyage back to 2036. I don't have the expertise to fully programme my machine, but like an aircraft pilot, I have some control of how I travel in it. My first trip, the return to 1975, was programmed for me so I could leave the machine to retrieve this portable computer. However, I will put in my debriefing report that anybody going back to a specific date should be aware of the type of clothing to wear. Back then they were in bellbottom patchwork jeans, suede fringed jackets, even platform shoes. I felt very conspicuous in this uniform."

Lucy was fixated on both Ian and John. Ian had overcome his initial shock and surprise and was conversing as though they were work associates.

"I've drafted up a drawing for a Time Travel machine," said Ian. "May I show it to you, I would value your knowledge?"

"You're welcome to show me, but I may be restricted with my comments as I explained a few minutes ago."

Ian turned to Lucy and asked her to fetch his laptop. She was careful to leave her smart phone silently recording. She quickly went to Ian's office to do as he asked. She was opening the file with his drawing as she walked back in. A sixth sense was telling her every minute with this encounter was priceless, possibly never to be repeated. She handed Ian the laptop just as the file was completely opening. Ian clicked on the 3D effect one and showed it to John.

"Be careful not to step into the portal," said John. "You can afford to lose a chair," he nodded to the support for his IBM computer, "but you don't want to travel through this portal until you're ready."

These words scared Lucy but Ian just seemed to make a mental note.

As John's eyes scanned Ian's drawing, for the first time Lucy noticed that they were almost completely black. She had a sudden ill feeling that perhaps they had materialised something they would not be able to control. Was this John character a genuine human from the future or a malicious entity from another dimension? Get a grip girl, she thought to herself, but she was concerned that Ian was not worried in the slightest. A few weeks ago she would have totally disbelieved anybody telling her such a tale, but the last few days had shattered her earthly grounding and now anything seemed possible.

The smart phone was still recording. Must get a photo she thought. Both Ian and John seemed intent their communication, so Lucy picked up her phone, pretending to take a call.

"It's Jim," she said. "I'll tell him we're busy and we'll see him this afternoon." Although the lab had CCTV cameras, they were placed to detect intruders at the main entry points; none were pointed at Ian and John. As she pretended to take the call she turned and took what she guessed would be good photos of John Titor. She had forgotten she had the shutter sound effect turned on and the slight whir and click could be heard. She froze. She had no idea what was standing in the portal. While it was a good possibility it was in fact the John Titor that she had come across in her research, what if it was some type of negative force? Lucy had gone through a phase of reading Alistair Crowley books and his claims of materialising devil spirits.

The click immediately caught John's attention. "You'll find that I will not show up on your photos other than as an indistinguishable dark shadow. If we are to have any further communication you must trust me and not be secretive.

Also the voice recording you're making will also only have Ian's and your voice being distinguishable. Mine will be at such a high frequency it will be inaudible when played back. Please do not take me for a fool."

Lucy was now terrified. Should she stay with Ian or go? She took a deep breath. "I'm sorry, John, I didn't mean to offend you. I hope that there will be no mistrust between us. But you can imagine that this whole experience is mind bending for me, and making me feel insecure, as all my normal special parameters are somewhat in disarray." She looked at Ian for support.

"Lucy knows who you are," said Ian, trying to smooth the situation. "She has done a lot of research and brought you to my attention. I believe that you stopped off in December 1999 but left again in January 2000".

"Yes. I wanted to see people's reaction to the Y2K Bug at first hand. That was part of my brief. We are about to encounter an even worse event unless we fix it, hence my time travel journey."

Lucy thought he was starting to sound more genuine now. Perhaps the black eyes were only from the ultra violet light emitting from the portal he was framed in. However he still was scaring the life out of her.

Ian interrupted her thoughts by again referring John to his Time Machine draft.

"Do you think that this will work?" he asked john directly.

"Well, it's very cumbersome and you don't seem to have a time specific date to programme in. How will you travel backwards and forwards in time?"

Ian outlined his Stonehenge concept.

John laughed. "Stone age controls for a stone age machine," he ridiculed. "But yes it will work in principal, if your supercomputers are smart enough."

Lucy was suddenly annoyed at the arrogance of this apparition or whatever it was. Ian was extremely smart and intelligent and she resented him being made a fool of.

Titor went on. "I can't tell you how my machine works, it's against the rules. But it was built by General Electric, after quite some time of research and development. I believe the boffins there reverse engineered a time mach…………

Suddenly the figure started to dematerialise as quickly as it had formed. And then he was gone.

"Damn!" said Ian, fiddling with the console controls. "I had lot's more to ask him."

"He scared me," said Lucy. "Do we really know what we're dealing with?" She didn't want to mention Alistair Crowley, but it was still at the forefront of her mind. There was something just not quite right about this John Titor and it frightened the life out of her.

Ian was looking drained. His face was ashen. Perhaps he had been too close to the portal. Lucy voiced her thoughts.

"I don't know, you could be right. Maybe next time I'll keep my distance. I've got a splitting headache. I'm off to my room, I'll see you in the morning." With that he left with an unsteady gate and his jacket draped over his shoulder.

Lucy was immediately concerned. This was not like Ian. He would have wanted to discuss all the aspects of what had happened and also see if the voice recording and photos were detectable. She grabbed her smart phone and stopped the voice recorder and replayed what had been recorded. John had been right. Ian's voice came and went as if one minute he was quite a distance away the next it was clear. Her voice was distinct but she had kept her distance from the portal. John's voice was simply a high-pitched sound that pierced her eardrums to such an extent that she had to immediately turn it off. She then thought about the photos she had taken. Again John was correct. His being was just a shimmering black mass, with no human shape whatsoever. The third photo stunned her. Ian's head stretched out towards the portal. The next was even worse. His head was a shimmering black mass, but still had the distinct outline of his head. What are we dealing with she wondered? There was slight panic in her thoughts. I should go and see if Ian's OK.

She knocked on his bedroom door. There was no answer. She tried again but louder this time. Still no response! She tried the door handle and it yielded straight away. Ian was spreadeagled across the bed. His jacket lay crumpled on the floor. She rushed to him. He had a faint pulse. She lifted his eyelids but his eyes were rolled upwards almost out of sight. She tried slapping him on the face, then went to the bathroom and got a cold wet towel and placed it on his head.

"Come on Ian! Wake up!" She was now in a panic, shaking him. At last she could hear a muffled groan. Slowly he was regaining consciousness. After a few minutes he could sit up. She poured him a stiff whisky.

"What happened?"

Lucy related the whole saga, but left out the Alistair Crowley bit.

"Ah, well, he answered some of my questions." Ian was still is a daze.

"Listen!" Lucy raised her voice for the first time since they had worked together, allowing her anger to get the better of her. "This could be bloody dangerous. *Children shouldn't play with fire*'. There's a lot of wisdom in that phrase." She said and she headed for the door. "I'll be in my room. Phone me when you're ready to discuss all the implications of this afternoon. And check the voice recording and photos I took," she said sharply, leaving her phone on the table.

He was still groggy, but managed to replay the voice recording, quickly turning it off when John had spoken, the shrill sound piercing his ear. He then looked at the photos she had taken.

Oh my god, he said to himself. What just happened to us?

# Chapter 8

Lucy had calmed down and felt that she should check on Ian again. If she phoned she knew how he would probably say he was, OK no matter how he felt. She went down to the canteen and got four packs of assorted sandwiches. She had just realised that she had not eaten all day and doubted if Ian had since she had left him.

She knocked on his door and entered. He was sitting on the edge of his bed still looking very pale. "How's the head?" she asked.

"Like a freight train has passed through," he answered trying to manage a smile.

"I'm sorry that I raised my voice earlier, it's just that I was worried about you. I'm also concerned that we don't really know what we're dealing with. Have we opened some type of Pandora's box? Jim phoned me earlier saying he couldn't contact you. I said you had a migraine headache and would be fine in the morning. Was that OK?"

"You've done a magnificent job, and held your nerve when John Titor appeared. I wouldn't have thought of recording it. I'm puzzled like you as to the exact entity we managed to materialise. I was too keen when we were talking to him to take an objective view. You are right to be careful."

"Did you notice anything particularly strange or out of place?" she asked.

"Well – the whole thing," he replied looking at her for some kind of sign.

Lucy said, "Well, where was his machine? If he is travelling in a Time Machine, no matter what it looks like it should have appeared with him in the portal. He was insistent that he kept touch of his IBM machine, so you would think it imperative that he kept his Time Machine even closer."

She looked at him as he allowed her comments to sink in. He was obviously still in some kind of shock. God knows what type of damage its done to his head, she thought.

She had struggled with herself about bringing up the negative entity aspect. She didn't want him to think her crazy, however given this afternoon's events anything was possible. She took a deep breath.

"Are you aware that on the fringe of science there is a perception of malevolent beings, perhaps in a different dimension, that appear when given the opportunity?"

"Like Ouija board," he ventured. This was not in any way his field, and normally would have no time for such trivia or what he would have called, nonsense. But he had a high respect for Lucy, and she had obviously ventured down paths, which to now had been too petty for him.

She continued. "Well along that track. I took a gap year after uni and dabbled in all the things students tend to do. I read the books of Alistair Crowley, and whilst not believing he could summon evil spirits, there are a lot of people out there who do believe, and practice Black Magic or Devil Worship. It has existed on the fringes since time immemorial. Over the centuries it has been recorded and handed down. There were John Dee's 17th Century Rituals, which are still practiced in secret today, and Anton La Vey's, *The Satanic Bible,* can still be found by those who know how. However I don't prescribe to any of this, and as a whole the thing scares the life out of me. But I do think that we should have a healthy respect for dark forces that we don't want, or understand. There was just something about John's eyes; they were pitch black. At first I thought it was just the ultra violet, but now I'm not at all sure."

Ian looked at her. Always full of surprises he thought. For the first time he was seeing her in a new light. Her anger earlier was out of a genuine concern for his wellbeing. He now realised he had been a bit blinded by John's presence and not thought it out like Lucy.

"What if we try again?" Ian said. "This time we keep our distance. How about we challenge him, challenge his identity?"

"I think that you were far too close. Can we operate the Collider from a safer distance, even if it's just a few feet?"

"No, we can't. But I can probably programme my computer to manipulate the important ones. We can start the Collider up, step away from the console and use my computer to fine tune the settings."

Lucy wasn't sure. "Listen we've said nothing to Jim. We promised to keep him in the loop. Maybe we should wait until tomorrow. You still look very pale and clammy." She passed him a pack of sandwiches and the both ate eagerly and in silence. Ian scoffed down the first pack and Lucy handed him another. They both had unusually elevated appetites. She had also brought down cans of Coke, which they dispatched in the same manner as the sandwiches.

"Let's get out of here," said Lucy, "go and get some pub comfort food and try to relax and re-group our thoughts".

"Sounds good to me."

Again there was a taxi waiting and Lucy asked the driver to take them to a bar that had good home style cooking. The driver nodded and within twenty minutes they had stopped in front of a quaint little bar. Not exactly what I had in mind thought Lucy, but they disembarked and Lucy paid the driver asking him to return in about an hour to take them back again. He nodded as he pulled out into the light evening traffic.

The bar was better inside than out and Lucy found them a corner booth. A young girl came up and offered the menus.

"What's the house speciality?" asked Lucy.

"Zurcher Geschnetzs," the girl said in a thick English accent. "It is thin veal strips in a mushroom cream sauce. It is my grandmother's recipe," she said this with pride. Obviously a family restaurant, thought Lucy.

Ian was very quiet. "Let's get some drinks as well," he said. Lucy stopped him getting up and went to the bar. She got a double whisky for Ian and a Vodka and Coke for herself. Their meals soon arrived on large oval white platters. Normally Lucy had a small appetite, but they both tucked in as if they had not eaten for days.

"Well," said Ian wiping his mouth with the large white napkin. "Where do we go from here?"

Lucy had brought a note pad. "How about we write down all the pros and cons." She had been taking charge since going back to his room and he was happy to let her continue for the time being. His headache had subsided but he was left exhausted.

"I think that we should go to Stonehenge as planned and get all the calculations done. We can then proceed to try to build your machine. In the meantime I think that we should not stabilize the mass again until we are better prepared. How soon that will be I don't know, but we can't afford a repeat of today. It could have killed you," She now looked dejectedly into his eyes, her compassion and caring obvious. He had to respect her opinion particularly as he had no better plan.

Ian now looked at her features as if for the first time. She was beautiful, he thought. He was starting to feel a slight attraction. The first emotions he had felt since Helen had died. Don't be stupid! You're far too old for her. She would never be interested in you, he thought.

"Well?" she said waiting for some kind of reply.

"I think that we should think very carefully before stabilizing the mass again. Do you think it was Jon Titor? Maybe we just couldn't see into the portal far enough to see if he had a machine. Or perhaps his machine is some type of backpack that we didn't notice." Lucy was relieved at this possibility. To be honest she did want it to be John Titor and not any of the other beings she had posited.

The taxi driver came back earlier than expected, but they had finished eating and were happy to go. Ian had slipped the girl his credit card when ordering the meals, and she duly brought the docket for him to sign.

Back at the facility Ian turned to Lucy. "I'm glad you're on my team, my right hand man, so to speak. I do value your input. How about we meet at seven in the morning to finalize a short term plan."

They said goodnight and went to their rooms. Lucy was a bit happier now that Ian was looking better. During the meal she thought that she caught him stealing a glance at her, perhaps in some type of romantic way. No! She thought. He wouldn't think of me in that way, more's the pity! She was really falling for him and didn't know how to stop.

# Chapter 9

The next morning Ian and Lucy arrived early to their offices. They had both had time to think things through since the disturbing events of the previous day. Ian had had time to consider Lucy's point of view and conversely Lucy spent her night thinking of the best way she could advise Ian on how to proceed.

"Hi," she said brightly as she entered Ian's office. "Hope you slept well. You look a lot better than yesterday. How's the head?"

"A lot better thanks," he looked up at her a bit sheepishly. "I suppose in hindsight, I should have taken more precautions." He added 'in hind sight' to try to regain his status. It wasn't necessary as Lucy immediately apologised again for her angry outburst.

"I think that we should go to Stonehenge as planned, it's only a couple of days away. That will give us time to assess what we've discovered to date. Besides Jim said that we have to wait to book more time on the Collider."

Ian wondered if Jim was bowing to pressure from other teams for time access, or if he was playing for time — trying again not to make any difficult decisions.

"You're right," he said, "we'll go on Saturday as planned. Are all the arrangements confirmed?"

"Yes. I spoke to your cousin Andrew last night and he'll definitely pick us up. Our lodgings are also confirmed. The surveyor, a Bruce Arrol, will meet us on site. I have his mobile number just in case."

How about we take the day off tomorrow?" Ian suggested. "I think that we both need a rest."

"Great Idea," Lucy agreed. "I have a taxi booked to take us to the airport at seven Saturday morning. The Solstice is on Monday morning, so we'll have plenty time to set things up when we get there. It's only just under a four hour flight."

After a pause, Lucy added, "Oh! One other thing! For the past few years there has been 'open access' to the stones on the Summer solstice. In Druidry it is called 'Alban Hefin' which means 'Light of the Shore'. Druidry has a great respect and reverence for the place that is considered the Between Worlds —hence the name Seashore where the Earth, the Sea and Sky meet. Up until last year everyone was well behaved and Heritage England allowed them access to the stones to worship as the Druids believe has been done for millennia. But last year a radical group intent on causing trouble started to riot and the whole thing was bedlam. Some of the stones were defaced, so we will be the only people granted access this year. There will be a large crowd behind the fence though."

"Always full of interesting information," Ian smiled. She never ceased to amaze him.

* * *

They met at the entrance on the Friday morning as planned. Both had carryon luggage only. They didn't mention the events previously experienced regarding the John Titor episode. It was like an unspoken rule. The flight was uneventful Ian fell asleep. Lucy didn't wake him when his head rested on her shoulder. Lucy was pleased to feel his closeness. She had breathed in his aftershave. She loved the distinctive aroma. The flight attendant woke him just before landing. He felt a bit embarrassed but neither of them said anything.

Andrew was there to meet them as promised. Lucy could see no family resemblance. Ian had said he was on his mother's side. She sized him up as the cousins exchanged greetings. She got the impression that they were not close, but Andrew had gone out of his way to be helpful. She marvelled at the English countryside as they sped off to Salisbury. Andrew avoided the motorway to make the journey more interesting. She was content to sit in the back as the cousins chatted aimlessly. After about an hour they were at the Arms Lodge. Heather had been right. It was a seventeenth century mansion set in beautifully manicured lawns and well kept gardens. There was even a small lake with weeping willow trees, their leaf-laden branches leaning to kiss the water. How romantic, she thought.

Ian was still in conversation with Andrew as they made their way to reception. She could see the small bar where old paintings graced the walls that extended to a lounge area.

Lucy introduced herself to the girl who was smiling behind the desk. "Heather, I presume?"

"Yes," was the bright reply. "Your rooms are ready. Twenty, twenty-one and twenty-two, all up on the first floor! I'm sorry. We don't have a porter to carry your bags. We're a bit short staffed today." Lucy nodded and directed Ian and Andrew to the stairs. She had taken room twenty and gave the other two keys to Ian. Please take twenty-one, Ian, she thought to herself.

Ian had enjoyed the panoramic views as Andrew drove, pointing out places and sights of interest. He had never been to this part of England. The White Horses carved out from the rough hillside turf to reveal the white chalk underneath were particularly impressive.

"Heritage England keeps the site clean, but what you see is probably three centuries old," Andrew had told him. The abstract horses were probably sixty feet high and dominated the landscape they were travelling through. Lucy had been quiet in the back seat. Ian wondered if it was because he had fallen asleep on her shoulder. Had he crossed some kind of line? He was annoyed with himself. And even more so because he realised he had felt a pang of jealousy when Andrew had tried to flirt with her as they arrived at the airport. She either hadn't noticed, or chose not to. He was behind Lucy as they climbed the stairs, trying to avoid the very feminine curves he was faced with, again rebuking himself for having any thoughts of intimacy. He did, though, deliberately take room twenty-one, knowing that he would be close to her.

They all met downstairs at about the same time. Andrew had invited the surveyor, Bruce, to meet them to discuss exactly what they had planned. Bruce looked initially at bit surprised. He wondered why any one from CERN would want a specific time continuum to be measured in such a way. But he was being paid more that his usual fee.

"I wonder if we can go down there today to see what's involved?" Ian suggested. All were keen on this idea and they went off in Andrew's car with Bruce, sitting beside Lucy in the back. He tried to ask questions regarding his selected task only to be met with her questions of his knowledge of Stonehenge, which as it turned out was very little. They both chose to sit in silence as again Ian and Andrew did all the talking. When they arrived the car park was full. Andrew showed his permit to one of the attending police officers.

"Are you sure that you cannot come back at another time? Trouble is starting to brew already. Access to the sight has been denied and a lot of people are angry."

Ian looked at the crowd, now beginning to face them. These were not Druids he thought, more like new age hippies intent on their perceived rights.

"We want to examine the sight so that we can have all of our instruments in place for Monday morning." Ian was addressing the policeman who was now being joined by another two. The police officers conferred amongst themselves then guided Ian and his party to what was now a fortified gate. Extra fencing was in place. Ian noted the fence hire stickers on the six-foot-high barrier that now surrounded the site. Normally a three-foot-high fence was enough to keep people out of the immediate proximity of the stones, and Heritage England normally only employed 'Information Officers' to ensure people respected the site.

Lucy grabbed Ian's elbow. "Do you think there's going to be trouble?" She asked, "Heather told me there was rioting last year. This crowd seems quite hostile."

He looked at the crowd. He had seen much more menacing sights at football matches, but this crowd was much smaller. "Just ignore them." He put an arm around her shoulder in a protective manner. They got some boo's from the crowd as they entered the gate.

Bruce seemed oblivious as he paced around the stones taking out a pocket gauge and lining up the heel stone through the capstones as he walked. When he felt that he had an accurate reading, he took what looked like golf tees from his pocket. "My instruments must be perfectly aligned," he said to the small group now at his side. He again checked his alignment and moved one of the markers a fraction. He nodded with satisfaction. "That's all we need," he said pocketing his hand held gauge. As they left through the gate they were again booed, one of the crowd shouting insults.

"It will only be worse on Monday morning," said the police officer who had initially met them. Are you sure you can't leave all this until another time?"

"Quite sure," replied Ian firmly.

With that they left in Andrew's car. Some of the crowd were banging on the bonnet and roof. Lucy was quite scared, but didn't want to show it. Ian seemed unfazed.

When they got back to the Arms Lodge it was late afternoon.

"Let's meet for a meal tonight. Where do you recommend?" he asked looking at Andrew.

"There's the Wheat Sheaf Restaurant in town. I drew the plans for the renovation from an old flourmill. Good food, and we'll be well looked after."

Ian looked at Lucy. "Sounds good to me," she said.

They all went their separate ways agreeing to meet at the downstairs bar at seven. Lucy dropped onto her bed. She felt exhausted. She noted Ian was looking pale again and worried about the after affects from their encounter with the Collider the previous Thursday. I'm glad that we came away, she thought. We both need some time out.

Ian was lying on his bed reflecting the same thoughts as Lucy. He really wanted to talk to her, but wrestled with what he saw as temptation.

# Chapter 10

The Wheat Sheaf restaurant was quite large with seating for about a hundred. It was themed on the old flourmill that had been the building's earlier life. The grinding stones set at ninety degrees to each other had been retained. Sacks, stencilled with the word 'flour' were stacked to one side. The old water wheel was still turning, featured behind a large glass panel. They were close to a river and a sluice trough had been formed about a metre wide. This was what turned the wheel. Andrew told them that the original intention was to have the grinding wheels still in action, but the noise was so deafening it was not conducive to a relaxed restaurant atmosphere. So the compromise that evolved was quite effective. On the adjacent wall a monochrome mural had been painted depicting the mill and it's activities at in the late 1800s. Lucy loved the old steam driven truck emerging from the far corner.

"Who did the art work?" asked Lucy turning to Andrew.

"It was a local named Slavco. His family were from an Eastern European country but he was pretty much brought up here. He's done an excellent job of capturing the activity of the time." Lucy and Ian both absorbed the whole scene with admiration. "He does all the hand written signage I need done." Andrew continued at the same time glancing at the wine list. It was only the three of them as Bruce had gone home to his family.

"Any particular wine you'd like?" Ian looked at Lucy and they agreed that Andrew should choose. The wine was ordered and also the entrees. Andrew had enjoyed his, obviously having had it before, but Lucy noticed that Ian pushed his around his plate unsure if it was lack of appetite or just not to his taste.

Ian had noticed that Andrew was quick to finish while Lucy was slow. Andrew was trying to draw her into conversation, which was becoming more of a flirty nature as the evening went on. They all enjoyed their main meals but Ian was keen to get back to the Arms Lodge. He was annoyed at his cousin's continued attempt to flirt with Lucy, even though she was doing nothing to encourage it. God, he's a married man, thought Ian. Leave the poor girl alone! He then realised the possible hypocrisy of his thoughts, as his jealousy had not abated.

They went straight back to the Arms Lodge where Andrew suggested after dinner drinks. Ian declined saying that he was exhausted, Lucy also declined for the same reason. "I'll have a couple before retiring. See you both in the morning." Ian and Lucy nodded and headed up the stairs together.

"Listen, Ian. I have not invited Andrew's constant flirting. It's getting a bit difficult to deal with, but I suppose it's only for a couple of days."

"Sorry, Lucy! It's a bit difficult. He's always been a bit like that. I'm sure he wouldn't want you to feel uncomfortable. I'll have a word with him if you like," he looked at her.

"God, no!" she said quickly. "I can look after myself. I just didn't want you thinking that I was leading him on in any way. As I said, it's just a couple of days."

"It's Sunday tomorrow, our last day before the survey. Andrew offered to drive us around. What do you think?" he said.

"No," she said. "Not for me. I'll wander through the beautiful gardens they have here and just take it easy," she replied.

"OK, then. See you in the morning for breakfast, about eight?"

"Yeah, fine," she answered as she turned her room door handle. "Good night!"

They had both felt some kind of chemistry between them at that moment, but neither had voiced their thoughts. She was now disappointed that Andrew was here. She had enjoyed their nights out together back at CERN, now this bloody Andrew was starting to get on her nerves. Wish I'd booked a different hotel for him, she thought to herself. Meanwhile, next door, just a few feet away Ian was having similar thoughts. I wonder if it would have been any different if we had just been on our own. He was starting to sense that she had feelings for him. Was that really the case? Should he admit to her that he was aware of feeling a building affection? They both went to sleep with their thoughts resounding in their heads.

They all met for breakfast as arranged and Andrew mooted the offer to drive around sightseeing. Ian reluctantly agreed but Lucy feigned a headache and returned to her room as soon as they had eaten. Andrew had no idea of the John Titor encounter, and Ian had no intention of telling him. However, because of their secrecy, Ian put on a brave face as again Andrew drove around the County. It was certainly rich in heritage and Ian did love seeing the canal barges, now converted to houseboats, or long boats, as they were now called. He loved the Romany style artwork that was endemic in the travellers' life style, which was now quickly disappearing. Andrew invited them out for a meal again when they returned.

"I'm not that hungry," said Lucy, "and we have a big day tomorrow."

"We could go down to the local pub and get a counter meal," Andrew suggested. Ian looked at Lucy and she nodded. The pub was a building in the Tudor style with whitewashed walls and the distinctive black wooden beams angled and crossed in distinct contrast. The roof was thatched and jutted out over the walls. 'The Poacher's Pocket' was written on the swinging sign. A picture of a stooped poacher with oil lamp and dog by his side, and a pheasant protruding from his pocket was exquisitely hand painted.

"Another of Slavco's works?" she asked.

"Clever girl, spot on."

Don't patronise me, she thought, but gave a faint smile in response. They each had the 'all day' ploughman's lunch, with both Lucy and Ian refraining from any drinks. Andrew though, managed to down a few pints of larger. The conversation had become slow and Lucy took charge by saying that she still had a headache and suggested they leave now. Ian readily agreed, Andrew mumbled that he would have a few more drinks back at the Arm's Lodge.

They left Andrew in the bar. As they climbed the stairs, Ian said, "Big day tomorrow".

She looked directly into his eyes, tilted her head and drew him close to her. With this encouragement he kissed her. It was a long passionate kiss. They were both lost in it until they heard voices at the bottom of the stairs.

"Would love to invite you in, but just now is not the time," he said, gently untangling himself.

"Yes, I know," she said. "I hope you don't think I was being forward, but I've been growing attracted to you for a while."

"Don't worry, me too," he reassured her. "Plenty of time when we get home, or should I say back."

"No, I like home," she smiled at him. "See you in the morning."

"Sure will! Meet you at 3.30. We need to be there in plenty of time."

She smiled again and entered her room.

They were all up and ready at reception. Andrew looked a bit hung over, Lucy thought.

"Sunrise is 4.38," Ian said. "Let's get going."

When they arrived they could make out a huge encampment, and lights inside a multitude of tents. "Hope we don't have the same trouble as last time," Lucy voiced her concerns. They went directly to the gate. The same police officer was on guard.

"Sure you want to proceed?" he asked.

"Yes," said Ian. "No problem."

"Hope not," was the gruff reply.

Bruce turned on a bright LED torch, trying to find his markers. This had the effect of drawing attention to the fact that they were inside the perimeter fence. There was still twenty minutes until sunrise. Bruce was focused on his work. This time he had his whole surveying kit. The scope rested on a tripod, and Andrew was at the heel stone holding a red and white marker pole. They both had walkie-talkies and Bruce was relaying instructions to Andrew. The amplified voices were drawing the attention of the quickly growing crowd. There was a lot of booing. Lucy could see that there were about twenty police officers and they were far outnumbered by the growing and ever aggressive crowd. There was a faint light grey on the horizon.

The sun was about to rise. Bruce was busy giving Andrew last minute instructions. Lucy looked in awe, as the first rays of the sun appeared to rise above the stones. There was cheering and booing. The crowd seemed divided. Many were just happy to enjoy how spectacular the sight was, even from outside the fence, but a growing crowd, shouting abuse and jostling with police was now becoming very rowdy.

"Don't let them spoil the moment," said Ian. "It's not every solstice that the sky is so clear." He seemed unconcerned about the aggression of the crowd. Ian tried to say something to Bruce, but he held an arm up showing that he must not be disturbed at this critical moment.

Lucy and Ian kept looking in awe at the spectacle before them. The sun had risen between the capstone and heel stones. Even though now out of perfect alignment, it was incredible to think that a people four thousand six hundred years ago had the knowledge and insight to build such a monument.

The moment soon passed. It was fully light and Ian was now worried about the angry crowd. One of the police officers had accompanied them into the fenced off area, but this was not much comfort as the crowd was now angrier than ever, feeling that they had to forgo their right to access the stones. Ian did notice that none of them seemed like Druids; they appeared to be just angry students. He voiced this thought to Lucy.

"We were students once," she said, trying to put a brave face on things.

Ian went to the gate where most of the police officers were. He stood in conversation as the crowd started throwing things. Lucy was now terrified.

Ian returned. "The police will form a cordon around us to the car. They say we should leave now." There was no argument from Lucy.

Stones and other missiles fortunately missed them, as they went through the gate. The police provided an escort towards the car. Bruce was huddled up, protecting his fragile equipment. Andrew carried the tripod and marker pole. They managed to get to the car. Just as Ian was getting in a stone hit him on the head. Blood was now running down his face. Lucy looked at him in horror.

"Go, Go!" a police sergeant yelled, trying to control the situation.

Lucy's tears were evident when she looked at Ian. There was a gash on his forehead and his shirt was covered in blood.

"Looks worse than it is," he reassured her.

The crowd was now banging on the bonnet and roof. One young man had hold of the windscreen wipers. Andrew accelerated, and then sharply applied the brakes. The figure went flying forward, one wiper still in his hand. They managed the getaway, the noise probably the most frightening.

Ian turned to Bruce when they were clear of the site. "How did you manage? Did you get all the readings that we need?" Bruce smiled and held up his scope and some kind of recorder like a smart phone.

"All here!" He indicated his survey scope as if it were some kind of trophy for work done.

Ian had no thought for his head wound. He just couldn't wait to get back to compute all the work Bruce had done.

# Chapter 11

Ian and Lucy were back at CERN. The trip home was uneventful. Both were keen to examine Bruce's surveying work. It was all held on a small memory card. Bruce had explained that he had surveyed the exact position of the heel stone's point, as it would have been on the Summer solstice four thousand odd years ago. He then had surveyed the difference as it is today. Although ravaged by time the point of the stone could still be ascertained. The gauges he had used were state of the art; a theodolite with an automatic 3D scanner and lasers. Using smart phone technology, he had managed to survey the four thousand-odd year difference of the two Summer solstices to a millionth of a degree. Now all they had to do was to feed the information into the facility's super computer. Unfortunately, neither Ian nor Lucy had the computer expertise to do this, so they would have to alert someone new to their discovery. To this end they were now sitting in Jim's office trying to seek approval and requesting computer time and a technician to help. Jim though, was off on another tangent. He was still unaware of the John Titor incident. His main focus as they sat there was their Stonehenge expenses.

However, Ian seemed to have the ability to change the subject by answering questions with a question. This always confused Jim, much to Lucy's amusement. After much discussion, the expenses being forgotten, a time was agreed for computer access.

"I've managed to get them to allocate you Mark Davidson. He's young but very bright. Word has it he hacked into the CIA, NASA, and the White House's mainframe computers before he was caught. It was decided not to punish him but to use his abilities to keep the CERN computer firewall safe from attack. To date he's been very successful. Of course his duties are all confined to the computer block. I'm confident that he won't discuss any of your work. He'll meet you this afternoon at two o'clock. I've arranged for your passes and swipe cards to be ready. Keep me in the loop, won't you."

"Of course," said Ian, looking Jim directly in the eye.

Cool as a cucumber, you've got to give him that, thought Lucy. They did not let their feelings show at work, but Lucy longed for a chance for them to be together. He had held her hand on the plane during some very bumpy turbulence, but time had not allowed them the private space she craved.

They signed in at the computer block, a huge building set alone in the facility. Security was tight, but even more so here. They were duly handed their ID and swipe cards. Their handprints were already on the facility's records. The guard at reception dialled an internal number, saying something inaudible when he was answered.

"Take a seat, he won't be long." The guard motioned to the row of armchairs in the reception area.

Within a couple of minutes a tall young man emerged from the lift and walked towards them. He was nothing like Ian or Lucy had anticipated. They had thought of a geeky spotty faced student type. But this young man was well presented, even sporting a shirt and tie.

"Hi, I'm Mark." The friendly voice was welcome in such an overwhelming building. They shook hands and exchanged pleasantries. "I'll show you the mainframe computer, then we'll go to my office. We can discuss your requirements there, where we won't be disturbed." They went through the security doors then climbed a flight of stairs. Mark opened the door, and they were faced with a towering mainframe, encased in glass, with access doors and a platform on each floor. It was six floors high.

"Why is it encased in glass?" Lucy asked.

"It works on a binary system of course, and when in full use it is like gates opening and shutting with ones and zeros. It does this at such a fast pace that it generates a very high heat. So it is behind the glass with cooling fans to keep it at a stable temperature. Without them it would literally melt."

"My laptop gets hot, is that for the same reason?" Lucy asked thoughtfully.

"Yes. But this is a supercomputer. When you run the Collider it takes ninety nine percent of its power. That's why we have to know when the Collider is being used and times have to be booked."

Lucy looked at Ian. He had the same thought. "Mark, do you keep records of the computer's performance?"

"Yes, of course. Why, do you ask?"

"Do you have the record for last Thursday, the seventeenth of June?"

"Let's go to my office," Mark suggested.

He gestured to them to sit opposite him at his desk. He turned his desktop on and within a minute he had zigzag charts on screen. He kept scrolling back.

"Here we are," he said turning his monitor so they all could see. The zigzag had suddenly flatlined. There was a time code in the bottom left hand corner. Its hours, minutes and seconds were still spinning round, but the Collider seemed at rest.

Ian recognised, as did Lucy, that this was the time John Titor had arrived. "What does that flat line mean?" asked Ian.

"Hoping you could tell me," Mark replied. "I've been waiting for you to come back. I learnt a long time ago about office politics and pecking orders. I just work here by myself. I noted that you had the Collider booked. When I was asked about it, I lied that the French had had a power surge and everything went down. Sometimes we have to draw power from the French grid, as the Collider chews up so much electricity. So I'm at your disposal by request, but it would help if I knew the truth. You can trust me, I think that I've proved that."

Ian looked at Lucy. She nodded her approval. So Ian related the John Titor incident exactly as he had remembered it. He left out the short-term damage it had done to his health. Lucy, feeling that Mark should have the full picture filled in the gaps, especially the audio and photos. As an afterthought she mentioned their unusually large appetites. It wasn't until she recounted it that she realised just how hungry they had been.

Mark nodded without an interruption, as they both recounted the story. When they had finished he looked at them both.

"I can give you my opinion for what it's worth."

"Please," said Ian. Lucy nodded in anticipation

"I'm actually aware of John Titor, whom I do believe time travelled back to 1975, then stopped off in 1999/2000. I also believe that he stopped off when we built the first viable Time Machine, as cumbersome as it may have appeared to him. So yes, it is quite possible it was John Titor, but, and there is a big **but**.

"You say he had no visible Time Machine. No matter how advanced, it would have to be big enough to comfortably encapsulate him. I think that, either he's waiting for you to build your machine and only partially materialised, or it was an inter-dimensional entity. They can be like naughty children and take on any form that they want. Of course that's only an opinion, given from what I've read on government computers. Black ops agencies do track this sort of thing. I only know because I hack UK and US 'secret' files. If I tell anyone then I'm open to arrest under probably trumped up charges. So I sneak in and out. It's all very interesting if you're into that sort of thing."

Ian seemed to be summing up what this young man was telling them. Lucy was a bit in awe that he was so matter of fact about the whole thing.

Eventually Ian spoke, "OK, what you say makes some sort of sense, but what about the photos and huge increase in appetite?"

"Well, it's obvious that your body was vibrating at a much higher frequency. So was Lucy's, but she wasn't quite as close to the wormhole. If that's what it was, and I'm sure it was, the body's atoms are adjusting to the other dimension. This has the effect of increasing the metabolism, affecting your DNA. The sudden metabolic change will, by its nature, increase your appetite. This is why I don't doubt your story, but we do have to figure out exactly what you did materialise. When do you have the Collider booked again?"

"We don't yet," said Ian. "I need this survey data taken at Stonehenge run through your computer to extract a time specific time continuum to feed into the machine we intend to build.

Ian handed Mark the five-gig memory card.

Mark pushed the small black card into an adapter slot and brought all the readings up on screen.

"Bruce the surveyor assures me it's taken with state of the art equipment."

Mark studied the graphs for a few minutes. "There is enough here to give you a time specific timeline. He's done a great job." Mark was superimposing graphs on one another. "I'll have all this sorted out later this afternoon." He half looked up at Ian, obviously now deeply engrossed in his work.

"Mark," Ian said sharply to get his attention, "we haven't told anyone about the John Titor incident. We need to keep it to ourselves just now."

"What incident?" said Mark, smiling. Ian instinctively knew he could trust this young man, wise beyond his years.

# Chapter 12

Mark had completed the information as asked. He had loaded it to a small terabyte hard drive. He was now in Ian's office handing it over.

"There's plenty of extra space, I've a feeling that you may need it on your, as yet uncharted travels." There was something endearing about this young man, Ian thought.

"Do you have any practical lab experience?" asked Ian.

"In computers?" was the slightly puzzled reply.

"No. We want to build a Time Machine and we think that you're just the man to give us a hand."

"By 'we', you mean you and Lucy? How many people are involved if I may ask?" Mark obviously was keen, but wanted to know where he stood in the scheme of things.

"Well," said Ian, "yes, Lucy is fully involved and also, to a lesser degree, Jim. We are supposed to keep him in the loop, but what he doesn't know won't hurt him," he said this with a wry look on his face.

"I do have a degree in Engineering," said Mark. Full of surprises, thought Ian. Lucy had come in and Ian brought her up to date with the conversation.

"I do have a rough drawing for a machine," said Ian. "Perhaps you could take a look and see what you think."

"Where is it?" asked Mark. "From my office I can see everything that is carried out on the facility computer, I don't understand how I missed such an out of the box idea."

"I sketched it and used my personal computer, for just that reason. But I hadn't met you at that point," he said taking the sketches from his briefcase.

"What do you think?" enquired Lucy, as keen as Ian to make some progress. Her apprehension about the whole thing had lessened by that time, but the Stonehenge experience was still a vivid memory.

Mark studied the layers making up the machine. "If I could comment," he said looking up at them. "I fully understand your construction, and believe that, put together properly it could work. That's from an engineer's point of view, but what is holding the layers together? You mentioned it is a bit like the layers of a sandwich. If you equate it to a world globe turning on it's axis, the globe has a curved bracket to hold it in place at both the North and South poles." Mark looked up, looking for a reaction.

"Go on," said Ian, "I'm with you so far."

"Well I think that we can construct it. But we need access to the Physics labs. They have six floors. I can get the computer to give us access, restricted to only those you choose to nominate."

"You can do that?" Lucy questioned, not wanting to miss a second of the proceedings.

"Of course! If I can hack into Black Ops computers, this is child's play. You work in the Nuclear Physics side, right?"

"Yes," Ian answered "So?"

"We just make out that it has possible radioactive effects. No one will want to go within a mile."

"OK!" Ian asked, "Say we do build it, how do we get it out and to the Collider?"

"In parts," said Mark. "Each part is really innocuous. It's only when you put it all together that someone is going to ask what the hell you have."

Ian was thinking through the possible scenarios, whilst Lucy wondered what they were going to tell Jim.

"OK!" said Ian. "When do we start?"

"I'll dummy up a programme for the physics lab that no one will question." He looked quite pleased with himself. "I'll do it today. We can start tomorrow."

"Great!" Ian sounded excited. "What about ID and swipe cards for the physics lab floor we are going to commandeer? "

"Be ready first thing tomorrow. Anything else?"

Ian looked at Lucy. She shook her head. "No. We'll see you in the morning," he said with a smile.

Mark left then, and they looked at each other.

They had had no time to themselves. They had both missed the feeling of that first embrace.

"How about we take an early night and go out for a meal," Lucy suggested.

"Great idea! Can I leave it to you?" Then as we went off towards his room, "Six o'clock OK?" he asked over his shoulder.

Lucy wasn't sure whether to be pleased at his not questioning her ability to organise everything, or to be slightly disgruntled at being taken for granted. She chose to go with the former thought and smiled as she went to her room. This was now more than just two colleagues going for dinner; things had changed. What should she wear? What scent should she use? Her mind drifted through these thoughts as she showered and dressed.

Ian had lain down on his bed with a feeling of exhaustion. What Mark had said about his John Titor encounter made sense, but now he just wished he had more energy. He was going to have to keep up with Lucy. Had he made a mistake? Was the age difference going to be a barrier? Obviously she didn't think so. She had acted with total professionalism when at work, but he could always sense her closeness when she was in his office. It was different from before.

He had dressed casually and this time he was early. He waited at the entrance for a few minutes. He looked up as he heard the lift doors. She looked radiant. She had a new confidence as she strode towards him.

"Ready?" she asked. She had that alluring look that had first attracted him to her.

"Where to?" he asked.

"Wait and see," she replied as they emerged from the building.

The taxi stopped at quite a stylish looking restaurant. It's signage clearly stating that it was fine Thai dining. "Do you like Thai?" she asked.

"First time for me. But it smells great even from here." A young Thai waitress showed them to their table. Asians, always so polite, thought Ian. Lucy had Coconut Prawns but Ian was less adventurous with Peanut and Chicken Spring Rolls.

"Ever been to Thailand?" Lucy asked.

"No. But I have been to Cambodia, near the Thai border. They took a lot of shelling and bombing from the Yanks during the Vietnam War. The Ho Chi Min trail divides them, and some of it goes through Cambodia. Not a good time for anyone in that region, I guess." He wondered if his age was showing again.

"No. What amazes me is the fact that Vietnamese, Cambodians, and Thais are all so friendly. I think that I wouldn't be so forgiving of the West so quickly." She shrugged.

"Different culture I suppose."

They shared a Green Thai Curry with Jasmine rice.

"Really enjoyed that," Ian told her.

"Good! Ready to go back?" Ian nodded as he took out the taxi driver's card. Within ten minutes it was at the door.

Lucy snuggled up to him on the drive back. He enjoyed the feeling of closeness that he had missed for so long.

Ian said, "Lucy, I am really attracted to you and we seem to be forming some type of relationship. But," he paused, "I'm about ten years older than you, and...

"That doesn't matter," she interrupted him.

"Let me finish, please. It's eighteen months since I lost Helen and Ruth. Helen will always be part of my life. I can't pretend that she didn't exist." He wanted to clear this up before their relationship went any further.

"Of course. I wouldn't expect anything else." Lucy held him even tighter. "I realize that sometimes you will need your own space. Especially on old anniversaries, whether your wedding or her passing. You must tell me the dates some time, so I can be there for you or give you the space you need."

"OK. Thanks," he said.

They huddled together in silence for the rest of the trip. Not an awkward silence but something else.

The rain poured down as Ian attempted to pay the taxi. Lucy rushed inside while Ian fumbled to find the right money. He was soaked by the time he got inside the swing doors.

"Come up for a night cap. Get dried out before you get your death of cold," she said. He offered no resistance.

Up in her room he was drying his hair with a towel. She had taken his wet jacket and draped over a chair near the heater. Her room was tidy. Everything in its place, and a place for everything, he thought. Not like my room, glad we came up here.

She sat on the arm of the chair taking the towel to finish drying his ruffled hair. He turned to her. Their lips met. This time there was no one to interrupt them. They slowly made their way to her bed, the damp towel discarded on the floor.

# Chapter 13

Mark had everything ready the next morning as promised. He handed them the ID and swipe cards for the Physics lab. They had commandeered the ground floor. Mark had printed out the distinctive yellow and black radiation warning signs. These were displayed on the locked doors. He had also make a coin size sticker and put it beside the ground level lift button. He's thought of everything, thought Ian.

When they entered their newly acquired lab, Mark took out his laptop. He opened up technical drawings similar to Ian's sketches but much more professional and detailed.

"I've taken your drawings and put a lot of thought into the way we can build this to make it work, and also for it to hold together under whatever unknown forces it might encounter." Mark had detailed Ian's layers and modified the computer section with space-time continuum controls, which were from the Stonehenge survey.

He showed them the elevation, plan, and 3D precision drawings. Although choosing to follow an IT path, Mark obviously had excellent engineering skills. What he was showing them now was different from Ian's but had the same concept

"This 3D section is cut away to show how everything works," he told them. "I've devised a circular shell with a bigger dimension but only one eighth circumference. We can house the machine in it and keep it stable. The top and bottom of the housing has opposing magnets to that of the machine so there will be no friction. It will basically float. When the machine is friction free, it can be propelled without any resistance. The top and bottom of the machine's magnets will spin and propel it, while the middle of the machine stays stationary to its shell, if you get my meaning."

"Yes," Ian nodded his understanding. "You've done a great job in a short time. Is that the seating for the machine operator?" he asked.

"Yes. All of the parts will be too big to fit in the passenger lift, but there is a large goods lift at the other end of the floor. We can use it when we're ready to take it to the Collider. It will take us about a week to build it."

"I can help, but my skills are limited," Ian volunteered. "But you're the engineer."

""It's OK. I'll show you how you can help. You too Lucy," he said, turning to her. Up until now she had been engrossed in Mark's drawings and the technical detail, but was willing to help in any way she could.

"Just tell me what to do."

For the next week all three worked about eighteen hours a day. Ian and Lucy made sure that they stole time for each other. Sometimes Ian would stay all night in Lucy's room, while his own room became more and more of a mess. She had come to his room one night. She had tidied up while Ian sat and watched. She was quite happy to tidy his room and could feel his welcome gaze as she went. The more they were together the stronger his feelings for her grew. It was the same for her.

The machine took two weeks to build. Mark was a perfectionist and insisted on testing every component. If he wasn't happy, they would modify it until he was. Of course it could only be tested to a degree. They would have to create a mass in the Collider and then figure out a way to get the machine in. Ian discussed this problem with Mark as Lucy looked over his shoulder, her closeness obvious. They no longer tried to hide their relationship from Mark, so they were all comfortable working with each other.

"I've devised a slide for the machine to fit it into the Collider, similar to the slide in an MRI machine. It can be operated from a safe distance." He opened his laptop and brought up the drawing.

"I'm impressed," said Ian. "You and Lucy must keep a safe distance from the Collider while the wormhole is forming. And of course from whatever materialises. If I immerse myself fully into the wormhole and my body starts to vibrate at a much higher frequency, at least it won't be just my head giving me problems this time."

"I'm not sure about all this." Lucy was concerned after what had happened last time. "Can we not send a test object, rather than you going blind as it were?"

"Well you could try sending the machine with an object by setting the time and date, but there will be no one to programme the return journey. I can try to write a return programme, but we risk losing the machine." Mark looked at Ian.

"I'd feel a lot better if we did that." Lucy said, pressing Ian's hand, trying to get his undivided attention.

"Well, we've come this far. And it would be terrible to lose the machine." Ian looked at Lucy to reassure her. Then he turned to Mark. "What do you think?"

"I think that I'll write a software programme for an automatic return journey for the machine. After all we're going into an unknown. Even though the time continuum we figured out is, I believe, accurate to a week or two, we just don't know. The machine could even come back before we send it, had you thought of that?" He looked at both of them while he let his words sink in.

"Let's take some time out," said Ian. "We need to think this through very carefully. Also Jim has no idea what we're up to. Look, it's Friday and we've worked nonstop. How about we meet up again on Monday, here at seven am?"

"Sounds good to me," Mark smiled. "My girlfriend is starting to think I'm having an affair. I'm hardly at our apartment."

Ian and Lucy had not considered that Mark might be in a relationship. They had had each other and they could steal some time together. It must have been difficult for Mark. He had a room at the facility. Now they were finding out he lived mostly off campus. Poor girl, thought Lucy.

Ian and Lucy spent the weekend together. They were just enjoying each other's company. They went to a movie, even though it was in Swiss German, they welcomed the break and the time away from the facility. Much to Lucy's surprise and delight, Ian had booked a hotel room for the Saturday night. They made the most of the five-star room service and spent most of the time in each other's arms.

True to his word, Mark had written the programme for a return trip and presented it to them on Monday morning.

"I've never done this before, but it's the best I can do," he told them.

"I don't think anyone has done this before," Ian reassured him. He looked through the programme. Ian had basic programming skills, but found reading a programme a lot easier than writing one. He scanned all the lines that, to Lucy, were a tangle of words and symbols.

"This is the point of return," said Ian. Mark nodded. "How will the machine know it's reached its destination and it is time for return?"

Mark tried to answer Ian's concern. "The machine works on propulsion, right?" Mark looked at Ian who nodded his understanding. "Well, this bit of programming kicks in when it basically comes to a stop. It will sit for two hours and then retrace its time path, hopefully back to its time line point of origin."

"Why a two hour stop?" Ian asked out of curiosity.

"Just a preliminary stop off time. We can change it if you want." Mark looked at Ian for instructions.

"No, it's all fine I think. I suppose the biggest problem or issue is, will the machine stop in empty space. "What if it stops in the middle of a yet to be built wall, or under sea levels that are even now starting to rise?"

"I've programmed in outer sensors so it can't stop unless it's in free space."

"OK," Ian agreed. "Let's plan to get the parts to the Collider and finish it off. Are we all agreed we do a test run?" Mark and Lucy both nodded. "Right! Then I'll have to talk to Jim. I'll do it this afternoon."

Lucy asked, "Do you want me to come with you?"

Ian considered the pros and cons of her offer. While Jim could easily be distracted by a beautiful woman, he didn't know if he should allow her to be used in that way.

"Well, it would make it easier if we give him a distraction. If you wear that tight low cut blouse you wore on Saturday night it will certainly get his attention away from what we're about to do," he grinned. "Meet me outside his office at three, we'll go in together. That's as long as you're comfortable with the idea."

"See you at three," she replied with a mischievous look.

Ian had made the appointment with Jim's secretary and they were now standing outside his office. They were both trying to look confident. Lucy had dressed in a tight blouse with the top two buttons undone. God! I hope this goes OK, thought Ian. Jim's secretary buzzed through and they were ushered in.

Jim gestured them to sit down and Ian noticed that he was already ogling Lucy's cleavage.

"What can we do for you?"

"Well," Ian began. "Do you remember a few weeks ago, we thought that we could make a wormhole, thus allowing the possibility of time travel?"

"Yes, yes!" Jim was now more intent on Lucy than Ian.

"Well, we've managed to create a wormhole and, well it's a bit complicated," Ian stumbled.

Jim's attention was now focused on Ian. Jim hated Ian's cavalier approach to his work, especially as it was his, Jim's, Department and ultimately his head on the block.

"What do you mean complicated?" Jim was starting to get flustered. He hated anything that might be in any shape or form a problem.

Ian narrated the John Titor incident, the successful data from Stonehenge, commandeering a whole floor of the Physics lab, taking Mark on, and the building of their machine.

Jim was going darker shades of red as Ian spoke. "You were supposed to keep me in the loop," he blurted out. This was Lucy's cue to drop her pen and she slowly bent over to pick it up. Jim was unsettled on all fronts. He was angry with Ian, but realised that he had obviously been staring at Lucy's cleavage for far too long.

He tried to rally himself. "Is there anything else you haven't told me?" He stared at Ian.

"Well, yes! Lucy and I are an item." Lucy couldn't help herself. She took hold of Ian's hand as though it was the most natural thing in the world.

"Oh, yes!" Ian now looked directly at Jim, a challenging expression on his face. "We're going to test the machine tomorrow, so we need to book time. All day. We need to take the pieces of the machine to the Collider and assemble it there. Do you want to participate?" Ian's gaze was steady.

"God, no!" Jim almost yelled. "We haven't had this meeting. I'll book you time on the Collider, but if it all goes pear shaped, I'll deny everything."

Lucy bent over to pick up her bag as they left. She noticed Jim just couldn't help himself.

# Chapter 14

Ian had been up early, checking all the machine parts in the physics lab. He was making sure that they could transport the dissembled machine as easily as possible. They would have to go from the ground floor in the goods lift to the lower ground floor where the Collider was. Ian had checked and made sure that the Collider was booked for them. He noted that Jim had emailed a generic note to all department staff saying that he would be away for a few days and anything urgent should be sent to his secretary. No surprise there, thought Ian, doesn't want to be here if any problems arise.

An hour later, Lucy, Mark, and Ian were ready to transport the machine pieces. Ian had found a trolley, which they started to load. The sections were more awkward than heavy to handle. Ian was worried that the outer shell, the thing the machine would spin in, was too big for the lift. They left it till last.

"Here we go," Ian said, "let's see if it fits." They struggled to keep it upright as they eased it into the lift. Eventually they got it in, but there was no room for any of them to ride down with it. "Mark, go downstairs and wait for the lift. I'll press Lower Ground and jump out of the way."

It went as planned and Mark held the lift waiting for Lucy and Ian to get there. They manhandled the shell out and Ian accounted for all the pieces. "Can you deny access to the Collider, to anyone apart from us? Access denied to all other staff?"

"Sure can," smiled Mark as he quickly typed commands into his computer. It was already connected into the mainframe super computer, of which he had total control.

After two weeks of building and testing they knew all of the machine parts.

"Shouldn't take long to assemble," Ian reassured them. He was still following the Mark's diagrams just to be sure. Any mistake in assembly could take hours to rectify and they only had the Collider for the day.

Finally, they stood back and admired their handiwork. Mark had built the slide for the machine to enter the Collider. It had been too big for the goods lift so they had carried it down the flight of stairs, hoping not to bump into anyone and have to answer any awkward questions.

Mark plugged his laptop into the machine's computers. He was loading the return journey as planned. "It should go to 2036," he said. "With any luck it won't surprise anyone too much, if the John Titor character is to be believed."

"OK!" Ian looked at them. "Are we all ready to test this thing?"

They nodded.

It was Ian's turn to take over the operation. He started the Collider and waited as it reached optimum speed. Again he created a wormhole. Again it changed colours until settling on the ultra violet spectrum. Everything seemed OK. Then all three placed the machine onto the slide.

"Wait!" said Mark. "Just have to enter the return command." He skilfully and quickly finished his work and they all pushed the machine into the wormhole. Mark had devised a manual shunt for the slide, this way they didn't have to get too close to the wormhole. Lucy was worried as vivid memories of their last encounter came flooding back.

She was shaken out of this state as she now watched the machine start to vibrate. It glowed different colours of the rainbow until it reached ultraviolet. Suddenly it glowed from bright to dark, then bright again gradually it disappeared.

"What now?" Mark sounded matter of fact, as if what had just happened was an everyday occurrence.

"I guess we wait," Ian said. "You OK?" He noticed Lucy's worried look.

"Yes!" But her tone was not convincing. "Do we wait for the machine to come back? It was two hours we programmed in, wasn't it ?"

"Yes," Mark confirmed. " But it could come back in five minutes or sometime next week, we just don't know."

There had been much discussion as to what to send in the machine. Mark had wanted to strap a monkey in. Apart from the fact that they had no access to monkeys, Lucy thought this cruel and had voiced her objections. Ian had suggested a mouse. They could weigh it and record all its details and then compare the data when and if it returned. Eventually they had settled on a quartz digital clock calendar. Even though quartz was not as accurate as an atomic clock it was a better choice. An atomic clock uses electronic transition frequency, microwave and most importantly of all, the ultra violet spectrum. They all concurred Quartz was the best choice considering observations previously made. The ultra violet spectrum was very evident, making an atomic clock a questionable test object. So the quartz clock had been placed in the centre of the machine. Mark had asked if it should be strapped in, and Ian had agreed.

So the machine had been sent off to who knew where.

"I'm starving," Lucy said. "Can I get anyone anything from the canteen?"

"Sandwiches," said Ian, "and Coke."

"Me, too," said Mark.

She wasn't gone long. "My swipe card won't work," she said.

Mark looked puzzled. "I've programmed the three of us to have exclusive access. Everyone else is denied. It worked this morning, didn't it?" he quizzed her.

"Yes. I tried it three times just now. It's definitely not working."

Mark used a USB port from his laptop to log into the main computer. Ian looked over his shoulder.

"Something's wrong," he said as he feverishly tried to manipulate commands. He switched to voice activation, slowly and clearly speaking his commands.

"Access denied," the electronic voice replied.

Mark looked perturbed; his language would have turned the air blue. "Looks like I'll have to hack into my own system, perhaps my firewall is too good." These latter words were more to himself than to Ian and Lucy.

Lucy stood back. She took Ian's arm. "Do you think we're locked in?"

"No. Mark will figure it out," but he didn't sound confident.

"Give me your swipe cards," Mark said, and he scanned the bar codes with a smart phone, which was also connected to his laptop. "Should be OK now," he said, but Ian thought that his previous confident manner was now a bit edgy.

"What was the problem?" asked Ian.

"Just a glitch, all OK now," he replied without looking up.

"I'll come with you," Ian said to Lucy. They walked up to the door and Lucy tried her card again. This time it worked. She felt a bit relieved, but still concerned that they were at the mercy of a temperamental super computer.

They were both starving. They grabbed packs of sandwiches and cans of Coke. "Enough for an army," joked Ian.

Lucy was not as amused. It was as if the super computer was arguing with Mark. She voiced her thoughts, as they made their way back to the Collider.

"Just a glitch. These things happen," he said.

They were relieved to find that their swipe cards still gave them access. They shared the sandwiches and Coke with Mark. They were all ravenous.

"The vibration of the wormhole is affecting our metabolism as I said the other week," he said between mouthfuls.

Ian and Lucy nodded, both too busy eating to voice an answer.

"It's been an hour," said Ian after they had finished eating and drinking. Lucy was still hungry, but kept this to herself.

Mark was looking at the time on his laptop. "No, just thirty minutes," he said pointing to the date and time.

"Well my watch says an hour, and your date is wrong," Ian pointed to the left hand corner of Mark's screen.

Mark checked. He looked surprised. He went into the laptop programme features and opened the clock. He took Ian's wrist; adjusted the time and date and then clicked 'apply'.

As soon as he was back to his screen saver, the date and time were wrong again, exactly the same as they had been when Ian had pointed it out. Mark said nothing, but disconnected his laptop from the super computer access. He went through the same process as before. This time his date and time were correct. Both Ian and Lucy noticed the difference when disconnected from the super computer, but neither said anything. They now wondered how much they could trust Mark, or more to the point the super computer. Too much had happened for it just to be a glitch. However, they had to stay by the Collider to see if the machine returned.

Ian's thoughts were interrupted as the wormhole started to glow again with the now distinctive eerie ultra violet spectrum. They could see the outline of the machine as it vibrated with the colour. Gradually it materialised to a solid form. Ian used the remote slide to get the machine out and then shut the Collider down.

They all crowded round to see the clock. Two hours, just as we programmed, thought Ian.

Then he looked at the date.

# Chapter 15

The clock calendar was flashing 2038. Ian and Mark were puzzled. Where had the machine been? Could Mark have made a mistake programming in the date from 2036? It had been done in a hurry after all. Lucy didn't want to think too much about it. They were now in a realm that they basically knew nothing about. Children shouldn't play with fire. She heard the phrase repeating in her mind time and again.

"Look!" Ian said. "It looks like we have three alternatives here. One, the machine went to 2038 and the calendar stopped working while the clock continued to pulse out minutes and seconds. Two, while it was in 2038, perhaps someone was playing with the programming when it suddenly returned before they had a chance to complete what they were doing. Three, Mark made an understandable mistake while he hurriedly programmed the return journey. But surely the calendar should read this year's date?" He looked at Mark for his view.

"I don't have an answer. It's too late to check the program that was sent with the machine, so we can't tell if I've made a mistake."

"Why?" Ian interrupted him.

"Max is withholding the info." He looked sheepishly at his feet.

"Who the hell is Max?" Ian questioned, angrily. This was a side of Ian Lucy had not seen before. Not the tender loving man that she thought she knew so well.

"It's my name for the super computer." Again Mark was looking guilty, of what, was not yet evident.

Ian said, "Look, Mark, I think it's time that you were honest with us about this problem with Max. We both noticed the issue with your laptop date and time, and us being locked into the Collider. There's more going on here than you've let on."

"It's a long story," Mark said defensively.

"We're listening." There was no mistaking the authority in Ian's voice. When push came to shove, Ian was not a man to be messed with.

"A while ago I wrote *web crawler* programmes for Max. The idea was to crawl through the Internet. Also You Tube. At first all Max could recognise was a cat, which surprised me. But it has the highest hits on You Tube, Google Images, and Google main search. As Max learnt the faster his AI grew …"

"You mean Artificial Intelligence," interrupted Lucy. This was all getting too much for her. First the John Titor appearance and all the issues and questions involved there, then the fear of being locked into the Collider floor by a computer. Lucy was now confident that this Max was more in control than Mark.

"You lost control this morning with Max, didn't you?" she said accusingly. Her discomfort becoming more and more evident to her. She was in a situation that she could not control. The thought of a super computer with an ever-increasing intelligence was chilling.

"OK!" Ian was still trying to keep command of the situation. "Just how much control does Max have?"

"A lot! It's increasing every day. I didn't want to tell you, but Max wants to be part of our time travel experiment. He knows of the 2038 problem where time on all computers will travel backwards. The reason the recording of the John Titor appearance flat lined was because Max was sucking in everything in from the IBM5100 computer. The flat line was a screen so we couldn't see what was happening."

"When the hell did you find this out?" Ian's temper was now more evident than ever. Lucy was sitting in stunned silence. She was hoping that this was all a bad dream, but she knew it wasn't.

"Well, gradually this week. But the issues I had with the date and time and the swipe cards just underlined the extent of the problem."

"OK." Ian asked, "What would happen if we shut Max down and wiped some of his hard drives. The recent knowledge he has acquired, the AI if you will?"

"Can't! Max has given himself an override. I think that the issues this morning were him testing his abilities."

"That's why, when you unplugged your laptop from Max, you could reset your screen saver date and time without a problem?"

"Basically, yes," Mark admitted.

"There's nothing basic about it. We've got a super computer now taking charge, not only of our experiments but how and where we move in the facility. Who else knows about all this?" Ian was struggling to get his head around everything that was happening. There were too many dilemmas, for his very capable brain to deal with at one time. Lucy was frightened and had gone to Ian's side, trying to hold his hand for comfort. Even with all that was happening Ian managed to squeeze her hand to reassure her, as if to say, we'll work this out whatever it takes.

"What if we cut power to Max and turn the backup generators off?" asked Ian.

"Max would override it or just get power from the French grid which he's programmed to do if the Collider is using too much power. We can't shut down the French grid, we don't have the authority."

"OK!" Ian was thinking aloud. "We've got the machine date issue, to which you've posed a plausible answer. So we'll forget that for just now. We need to now focus on the problem of Max."

"He can hear what we're saying," said Mark. He was now wishing that he had never given so much authority to Max, even if it was inadvertently.

"I suppose he can bloody see as well," was Ian's sharp response.

Mark just looked at Ian. The look said it all.

"OK!" said Ian "That's enough for one day. Come on Lucy, we're going out for a meal. Let's take a break and discuss it again tomorrow."

"What about the machine?" asked Mark.

"Tell Max to look after it," he replied over his shoulder as he walked out with Lucy. She looked back to see Mark hastily typing commands, she presumed for Max.

"We're going back to that local restaurant we enjoyed so much," said Ian still holding Lucy's hand

"I'll have to get changed," she blurted out.

"We're going now!" She didn't argue with his authoritative manner, something she was finding attractive. She felt he was protecting her, the thing she needed most just now. She had tried to say something to him on the way out but he held her hand tightly indicating for her to keep quiet.

They got a taxi and Ian showed the driver the business card of the restaurant he had kept. As soon as they were in the cab, he relaxed enough to collect his thoughts and start to discuss things with her.

"The way things are just now, we have to assume that we're under constant surveillance at the facility. We don't know what Max wants, if anything. It may just to be kept in the loop. I think that there is one thing that Max doesn't have."

"What's that?" Lucy was eager to find a positive from the day's proceedings.

"Ego! I'm sure that Max cannot have an ego. It's a very human trait, I don't think that Max could have learnt that by crawling the net or You Tube. If he ever came across it as a written word, it literally wouldn't compute. We have to figure out a way to get Max on side, for now anyway, and any ammunition we have can only be a good thing." Lucy marvelled again at Ian's ability to manage in an adverse situation.

They soon got to the restaurant and quickly ordered a light meal. The ravenous hunger they had experienced earlier had dissipated.

"We need to regroup. We must assume for now, that anything we say at the facility is being monitored by Max. So we need a contingency plan." His mind was going at a fair speed of knots as he tried to figure out a strategy.

"Right!" he said decisively. "Ego is our first weapon as it were. What other weaknesses could Max have? In trying to match human intelligence, Artificial Intelligence attempts to replicate nature's coded behaviours that have been accumulated over millions of years. That would prove to be impossible. The human body DNA code alone occupies cubic miles of pages. Apart from genetic codes, nature has assembled similar volumes of code in a myriad of subsystems. I don't believe that Max has the computing power to match us.

"What do you think we should do?" Lucy was now fascinated and relieved that there could be an answer to at least one of their dilemmas.

"Try to give him the equivalent of a mental breakdown. Then, while in that state we take over and remove his recently acquired AI, but leave enough for us to still use him." He looked at her.

Genius, she thought. "How do we put the plan into action?"

"Phone Mark, tell him to come down and meet us. Don't give him any details, just say that it's urgent."

Lucy dialled Mark's number and went to the waitress to check the address of the restaurant. It was the same girl with the thick accent who had served them last time. Lucy gave her the phone so she could give directions to the restaurant. Retrieving the phone Lucy again told Mark to say nothing.

Soon Mark was with them in their corner booth, not that they needed the privacy as much as they had needed it on the facility campus. Ian outlined his thoughts. For the first time that day Mark looked relieved. Someone else was taking some steps to rectify his possibly foolish web venture with Max.

"Do you think that you can write a programme with enough data to overload him? We just need enough time to remove the relevant hard drives and to re-programme. Please don't tell me that he can read a DNA sequence in say five minutes, especially if you mix it with, say, that of a monkey. Max will have to unravel it; then find it's two different codes, then do as he's asked to define what the DNA sample is. Also, Mark, test his ego; I don't believe that he has any. Tell him that you do not think him capable. This will confuse him, as he will have to search his databanks rather than take umbrage as a human might. With all this overload, do you think he will shut down to self repair, allowing us to put his hard drive memory back to before you started messing with his AI?" Ian had obviously thought this through, but needed confirmation from Mark that there would be enough time to accomplish his plan.

"Yes, it can be done in the time frame. We just have to figure out what to delete, remember we needed him for today's work this morning."

"I didn't say it would be easy. I just want assurance that we are not going to create a bigger problem."

"No, we can do it. I'll figure out what to programme in tonight and put a time for completion sequence in, to overload him. We should have enough time to fix things, but I will need help."

"OK. When can we start? We need to fix this, and then figure out what to do with the machine. Perhaps send it on another test run. Jim's away, so we'll continue to keep the Collider booked for us. Can you do the open ended booking for us?"

"Yes. I'll do all the programming tonight. I'll need to hack into another super computer somewhere to get it all done."

"Whatever it takes!" Ian agreed. "I don't want to know. I'm sure you've got the skills for it. Just get us out of this mess."

# Chapter 16

By the next morning Mark had written the programme to confuse Max. He had had to hack into the French Metro Super Computer at night while it was basically on standby mode. Using the computing power he had done as Ian had suggested and mixed human and monkey DNA, then written the command to define what the sample was. All this was to be done within a five-minute time frame. This would be an impossibility for any supercomputer, thus causing it to melt down and self-repair. Mark calculated that the self-repair would take at least an hour. This would allow them to remove the relevant sixteen hard drives.

The hard drive of the super computer contained one hundred and eighty-two hard drive units, each of which had a one hundred and twenty-eight terabyte memory. These were wired in series, which was inadvertently giving them an advantage. Removing single hard drive units would ensure that Max could not respond when in 'self shut-down' mode. Mark had calculated which hard drives he needed to restore to a historical point before he let Max loose on the Internet.

This work was proving more time-consuming than Mark had calculated. After forty minutes he still had a lot to do and Ian was becoming concerned. Without the specialised knowledge, all Lucy and Ian could do was sit and watch. Mark worked frantically on each of the selected hard drives that he had removed. Of the one hundred and eighty-two, only sixteen were 'infected' with the AI Max had learnt.

The problem was that Mark needed to be very selective with the data being removed. Ian checked his watch. "Fifty minutes gone," he said to Mark, "you said we only had about an hour."

"Yes." Mark didn't look up as he feverishly typed commands to one of the few remaining hard drives to be restored. "It's taking longer than I thought, but if we don't plug any of the hard drives back in until we've finished I don't think that there is much Max can do. As I said they are wired in series, so leaving these ones out will limit his ability. The only problem is that he services the whole complex, and this will be affecting a lot of departments."

"Email a generic note to every department saying that the facility super computer has been shut down for an urgent upgrade and data protection installation. That should buy us time and allow us to finish. But do the email now."

"I don't think I'll be much longer."

"Send it now!" There was no doubt in Ian's commanding tone. "A lot of people will be wondering what's happening, so give them an answer."

Mark did as he was told, then got back to the hard drives. Eighty minutes had gone. Ian was worried but he didn't want to put any more pressure on Mark.

"This is the last one," Mark said, as much to himself as to Ian and Lucy.

Finally, the hard drives were ready to replace. Max had almost finished his 'self repair' but of course could not complete this task without the missing hard drives. Mark carefully plugged in the hard drives in the correct sequence. As he replaced the last one, Max slowly came to life. Ian had to admit that Mark had taken on a mighty task. He had to delete and keep selected data, no mean feat even for the brightest IT specialist.

"Wait a minute and we'll test his memory." Mark was now sounding more confident. Ian was glad to see this change in his demeanour.

"Go and check your swipe cards," he said as he watched his laptop screen. It was now plugged into Max. Lucy took all three cards and returned a few minutes later.

"All working OK," she said.

Mark addressed Max through his voice activation microphone.

"Hi Max. How are you? You were disabled for a while and you self repaired. Everything OK now?"

"Yes," came the electronic reply. "I managed to sort the DNA data you requested. It is a mixture of human and monkey. I don't know why it took so long. Is there anything I can do for you?"

Lucy thought that the electronic voice was eerie, and hoped that all of Mark's effort had rectified the Artificial Intelligence issue completely.

"Yes, there is. Our work on the Collider yesterday, what can you tells us about it. We will start communicating in encrypted format in written text until further notice."

Mark turned and explained to them, "I've got a software programme installed so we can communicate without anyone being able to listen in."

Mark was right to be cautious, thought Ian. He looked at the jumble of script on Mark's screen. It suddenly became intelligible as Mark typed in some prompts. Ian read the screen. Max relayed exactly what had happened with the Collider, but failed to mention the lock in and date time issue on Mark's laptop, which Ian noticed was now displaying the correct details.

"Ask him if he can hear throughout the complex, or only via a plugged in computer microphone," Ian asked, and Mark typed in the query.

Ian watched as the jumbled words appeared on screen, only to be coherent a second later.

"Only the security cameras and front enquiry desk microphone. The front desk microphone allows me to help staff direct visitors to their requested location," was Max's written reply.

"OK, thank you Max," said Ian. There was no response. Mark typed in Ian's words.

"You're welcome," was the encrypted typewritten reply.

"Let's go out for something to eat." Ian looked at both of them quickly making a 'zip' action across his lips. "First of all Mark, can you contact some departments at random to make sure that they have full working access to Max."

He watched as Mark ran his finger down the departmental extension list. Ten calls later Mark looked up smiling. "All report everything is OK, even thanked me for fixing the super computer issues!"

"Good. Let's go," said Ian.

Again a taxi was available at the main entrance. Ian directed the driver to the same restaurant. He couldn't be bothered to try anything else. He had more important things on his mind.

"How do we really know that we've re-programmed Max? How do we know that he's not fooling us?" Lucy was holding his hand as Ian addressed the question to Mark.

"I've deleted too much 'learned' information. He's programmed now to respond only to commands. Basically he doesn't have a mind of his own anymore." Mark's reply sounded quite confident. Ian wasn't as sure, but didn't have the computer skills to directly challenge Mark.

They all ordered their meals and sat in silence for a while. Lucy was the first to speak. "What do we do next? Should we try another test run with the Time Machine and the Collider?"

Ian said, "I could sit in and test drive it. After all, it did return within the prescribed two hours."

"No!" exclaimed Lucy. "It's far too dangerous."

"I'm willing to have a go. Like I said, it did return. Max confirmed he had all the information of the departure and return."

"Perhaps Lucy is right. Maybe it is too soon. Maybe we should do another test run." Mark was now voicing Lucy's concerns.

"We can't tie up the Collider for much longer. Jim will be back God knows when. I say we try it again tonight." Ian was being very assertive. Lucy was unsure how to deal with the situation.

"I still think that it is far too dangerous. Please reconsider." She looked at him with doleful eyes, trying to appeal to his sense of responsibility. After all, he should be thinking of her and their relationship, which had become almost matrimonial.

"We'll try again tonight!" He had a look in his eyes that Lucy hadn't seen before. She could tell that there was no way anyone or anything was going to stop him.

# Chapter 17

Lucy sat in silence as Ian gave instructions to Mark for the second test run of the machine. Obviously Ian wouldn't be there whilst 'travelling' so he wanted to make sure that Mark knew exactly what to do and how to stabilise the mass.

"Lucy will give you a hand, as she has been with me since we started working on this whole concept." Lucy wasn't sure how she felt about all this. Yes, she should feel flattered that Ian had such belief in her capabilities, but she still felt exasperated that he continued to ignore her pleas not to go. However, it was obvious to both Mark and her, that Ian was now hell bent on going, and nothing was going to stop him.

When they got back they went straight to the Collider. The machine was sitting exactly where they had left it. It looked precarious resting on the slide that fed it into the wormhole, but in reality its seating was quite firm. Ian was confident that his weight would not affect any of the loading procedures of the test run.

"Please don't go," Lucy tried again. But she knew that her words were falling on deaf ears.

Ian, ignoring her pleas, started his commands to create the wormhole mass. Lucy knew that she had to help Mark. She had the expertise that Mark lacked, and if Ian was going, she would do all she could to ensure his safety. Gradually the now familiar colour spectrum appeared. The hues melted into each other until the ultra violet spectrum steadied and glowed the eerie familiar shade.

"Programme the time settings as you did before," Ian ordered. Mark immediately obliged.

" What about the clock, do you want to take it with you?"

Ian pondered the question. What should one take to the future? Should one take some form of irrefutable time frame identity, so there would be no question where and when he was from? He voiced his thoughts. He was less frantic than before. A calm presence had come over him. Lucy wasn't sure quite what to make of it. She decided to let Mark and Ian decide on their current quandary.

"I think I should take the clock, but also something else."

"How about your smart phone?" Mark suggested.

"It's got photos of my lost family," said Ian. "Can I take yours?"

"Here! Take mine," Lucy said. "You've got a calendar, photos I've taken both here and Stonehenge. I would imagine Stonehenge is still standing. I photographed the surveyor, Bruce. You could always explain how we worked out time specific date for the machine."

"Yes, good thinking. Here, take one of us before I go." Lucy snuggled in beside him and took a picture of the pair of them.

The violet hue was still there, the mass stabilised, the wormhole beckoning.

"OK," said Ian. "Push me in."

Lucy shivered as she sat at the controls. Mark pushed the machine into the wormhole. It started to vibrate. Lucy could see Ian's form come and go and then turn to a silhouette.

And then it vanished.

Tears were running down Lucy's cheeks. She had a dreadful feeling that they had done something irreversible. Somehow she had lost Ian forever. She should have been more forceful, she thought. She looked at Mark. He was looking sheepishly at her, unable to find any words of comfort.

"We'll wait two hours and see if he comes back."

"What do you mean, if?" exploded Lucy, now unable to control her emotions. "Of course he'll come back!" But there was no conviction in her tone. Mark looked dejectedly at his laptop screen saver.

"There was no stopping him," he said, after a while. "His mind was made up. You saw him just before he left. Calm and cool, ready for the trip of a lifetime."

"You're not helping."

"I'll go down to the canteen and get sandwiches and Coke. I'm sorry, Lucy, but I'm starving."

"Me too! I shouldn't be, but I'm famished."

Mark was back fifteen minutes later. He had put a countdown stopwatch on his computer screen. "Ninety minutes to go," he said, trying to lighten the atmosphere without any success.

They ate the food. Lucy looked at the countdown. Seventy- five minutes.

"Do you think he's OK?"

"I'm sure he is." Mark tried to sound confident. "The clock came back undamaged."

"Yes — with the wrong bloody year. 2038, what does that mean? Where is Ian now? What year is he in?"

She was verging on becoming hysterical. Mark had no knowledge of how to calm her down. He had no sisters, had had very few girlfriends, and to make it worse she was probably right to be getting into such a state. He looked at the countdown. Just over an hour to go. "We could play a computer game while we wait," he suggested

"You must be joking," she spluttered the reply. "How could you even think of playing a game while Ian is out there somewhere. Do you know where?

"Well, no," Mark admitted, "but I'm sure that he's OK though. Look only forty seven minutes to go."

"It'll seem like an eternity," again tears running down her cheeks.

They sat in silence as the countdown continued.

Mark kept his eyes on the screen not daring to look at Lucy in case he inadvertently incurred her wrath.

Eight minutes he thought, should I tell her or wait until its one-minute. I'll wait, he confirmed to himself.

It did seem like an eternity, but finally the countdown was on the last ninety seconds.

"Just over a minute," he said to Lucy.

She turned to look at the wormhole. It was still stable, a shimmering ultra violet.

Something started to appear in the wormhole. "Thank God!" Lucy felt unable to contain herself. She would never let him do such a risky thing again.

A figure started to appear, Lucy was so grateful Ian had returned.

At first the silhouette! But there was something different yet familiar. Her mind was racing trying to process the imaging before her eyes. She glanced at Mark, but he seemed happy, a smile on his face. Obviously he thought all was well.

Gradually the figure materialised, sending shivers down her spine.

John Titor was in the wormhole frame, carrying the now familiar IBM5100.

# Chapter 18

Lucy stared in horror as the spectre of John Titor gradually came into focus. She was suppressing the urge to scream. Where was Ian? Why was this John Titor back? These were things that she had relied on Ian to answer. Now all she could do was stand transfixed. Mark was talking to her, but she wasn't listening, just shutting everything out. This was her coping mechanism. At last she screamed at John Titor.

"Where is Ian? What have you done with him?"

Mark was looking on, flabbergasted as the situation unravelled. He guessed he was looking at John Titor, who was now becoming a full entity as the shimmering ceased. The wormhole still glowed the same eerie ultra violet, which wasn't helping, he thought. What would Ian do in a situation like this? Mark was young and inexperienced, but he felt that someone was going to have to take control.

"Is this John Titor?" Mark asked Lucy who was now hysterical and screaming incoherently. He turned and slapped her face. This suddenly brought her round from the incontrollable state she had been in.

"I'm sorry. I didn't know what else to do."

He then turned to the portal. "I assume that you are John Titor." Mark was trying to speak with an air of authority, but it wasn't coming across that way.

"Do you know why I'm here again?" Titor asked.

"God, I wish you weren't," said Lucy. "We sent Ian to 2038 for two hours but you've come back instead. Where is Ian?"

"Where is the quartz clock calendar, it was in the time...."

They both suddenly realised that John Titor was not in the time travel machine that they had built. He was still standing in the wormhole, but there was definitely no machine to transport him. "We sent Ian in a Time Machine that we constructed. We showed you the plans," said Lucy. "Where is your machine?"

"It's underneath and part of my suit," he replied. We've made a lot of advances since the machine you built." He unzipped the front of his jumpsuit to reveal a panel with a blank screen. He touched it and it came to life to reveal a touch screen-type tablet. But this was flexible and was able to form around his chest. "General Electric still controls the market in this type of technology. There is a lot this tablet can do."

Mark thought of the first computers taking up a whole room. Now it could all be incorporated in a smart phone. It seemed to make sense.

"Why hasn't Ian come back?" asked Lucy, on the point of hysteria again.

John Titor looked at them.

"You messed with your super computer. You tried to erase all of its Artificial Intelligence including what it had learnt about the 2038 calendar computer bug. It learned this, and then you deleted part of it. So I've had to come back on a repeat journey to get an IBM5100 again. Do you know how dangerous it is for me to steal a portable IBM? Almost got caught. Imagine my defence. 'I'm a time traveller; just need the IBM for a computer bug in 2038'. I don't think so!"

Lucy was a bit calmer now. She had crossed her arms and she addressed John Titor directly. "Where is Ian? What have you done with him?"

"We've asked him to stay as our guest until we can get your IT expert to rectify the glitch that he or she caused whilst tampering with your super computer's memory."

"It was me....." Mark was not allowed to continue

Lucy interrupted with a vicious onslaught.

"You mean you're keeping him a hostage until we sort out this computer fiasco?" Her scathing glare went from John Titor to Mark.

"Well, I wouldn't put it like that." John had hardly replied when Lucy began another outburst.

"Mark, sort out this mess with Max. John, don't think that you can hold us to ransom. Mark here will reset Max, our super computer, to your specifications. But you let Ian come back right now!"

"Sorry, no can do. I have my orders." It seemed to Lucy that John Titor almost added a sneer to this remark.

"Yes, you bloody well can. Mark go and fix Max right now."

Both Mark and John Titor were replying in the negative at once.

"Shut up both of you. Just let me think." She was calmer now, trying to take control in Ian's absence. "Firstly. Mark, do you know what is required, and how long will it take?"

"I'll have to go back through my whole log of Max's reprogramming to find..."

"I can answer that," John Titor interrupted. "Do you have a terabyte hard drive with USB?" Mark nodded in the affirmative, pulling one from his draw. He quickly plugged it into his laptop and erased any memory it had. He handed it to John Titor.

John Titor pulled something from his pocket. It was a USB female port, some kind of adapter for his Time Travel tablet. Within less than a minute the data was transferred.

"I need to put Max to sleep to repair any damage done the other day." Mark looked dismal.

"No, you don't. Just plug that in through your laptop to your super computer and follow the prompts." John Titor seemed to be taking command of the situation.

"I want Ian back now," said Lucy. "You can see that Mark is following your orders. Though I don't see why you should be issuing any orders. Do you think that you are superior just because you've come back from the future?" It was Lucy's turn to sneer. She didn't like John Titor one little bit.

"I just have my orders. You wouldn't understand. I say that because you've never been part of an elite force, with a strict command structure. It's why we work so well." It was becoming a battle of wits and mental superiority and Lucy wasn't going to lose. She might not have military training, but she did have the mental discipline to get a PhD.

"Your IBM5100 looks heavy," she said to him. "Do you need something to lean it on? Why not come out of the portal and sit down." She immediately saw a change in expression. He was struggling to answer, she thought. Then it dawned on her. He was terrified to leave the portal. Was he scared that she would de-stabilise the mass and he would be stuck in time!" Why not come and join us while Mark completes the necessary computer adjustments."

"No. I prefer to stay here." He looked directly at her, but she could see through his bluff.

"You can only stay there for so long. You'll have to rest soon. I know how heavy that IBM5100 is. You could only hold it for about five minutes last time before resting it on the back of a chair. You've now been here, for, let's see, about ten minutes."

"Shut up," he replied. "You!" he addressed Mark. "Hurry up with that reprogramming."

"Going as fast as I can," said Mark oblivious to the revelation Lucy had made.

Suddenly Lucy shut the lid on Mark's laptop.

"Bloody hell, what are you doing?" Mark looked annoyed. He felt that he was almost finished. What was she doing?

"Well!" said Lucy. "Looks like we have a stalemate. Do you play chess?"

"No!" was the angry reply. Lucy knew that she that she was now turning the tables.

"This is what we are going to do. Mark will finish as soon as you give us the IBM5100. We will keep it until Ian comes back. As soon as he's back we'll send it to your specified date and time."

"That's not what's supposed to happen." There was almost a whine to his voice. The hardened soldier was now reduced to having to think for himself. He was trained to follow orders without question. He was not trained to think for himself.

"Looks like it's getting very, very heavy." Lucy pointed to the IBM.

John Titor glared at her. She could tell that his strength was draining and any minute he would have to put it down.

Lucy was now quite composed. She was quite prepared to play this mind game for as long as it took. And by the look of it, it wouldn't be long. She started humming to herself, her smile causing John Titor intense annoyance.

"Twenty minutes! Must be really heavy by now."

John Titor's features were grim. The blood vessels were standing out on his neck. He looked like he was about to burst. "OK," he said "Take this bloody machine before I blow a main artery."

Lucy moved forward and took the machine. She almost dropped it, it was so heavy.

I'm going to close the portal now. I will create a wormhole again in thirty minutes. I expect to see Ian. If not, Mark will not finish the super computer repair and you will have to find another IBM5100, though from what I've read, very few were built, so good luck with that."

She saved Mark's work and used his laptop to close the mass down. John Titor started to shimmer and vibrate as she deftly typed in the commands.

She could hear John Titor's discontented words, as he became a silhouette, then disappeared.

# Chapter 19

Ian glanced at Lucy as they pushed him into the wormhole. He was firmly strapped in, but was not feeling in the least bit secure. However, he did not let his feelings show; instead he looked ahead to avoid Lucy's pleading eyes. He started to feel bumps, like aircraft turbulence, but at regular intervals. This started to gain momentum as the colour spectrum changed towards ultra violet. His body was now feeling as though he had a jackhammer within his spine. He gripped the handles on the machine as the ultra violet shimmering started. He was about to glance at Lucy, when he saw a sudden flash of white.

"So you're Ian Sinclair. Do you know how much trouble you've caused?" A man in some type of military uniform was standing over him.

Ian's feet were planted to the floor as though glued. He couldn't move them, but there was no sign of shackles, rope, or any other form of restraint. He pulled at his feet; they were firmly fixed to the ground. Then he noticed that he was wearing some kind of boots. Relatively normal army issue type, nothing strange he thought. He tried to stand and take a step. He used all the strength he could muster. Pain shot through his ankles and calves as the boots were restraining any movement. He wasn't going anywhere. He thought perhaps he should be glad it was only his feet, as the rest of his body seemed to be free from any restriction. He looked up at his interrogator. There was something was vaguely familiar. He was in relatively comfortable surroundings, some kind of lab he thought. He looked up again. It was the insignia on the man's sleeve. The same as John Titor's!

"I'm ravenously hungry and my throat is dry. Can I get some food and drink?"

"Will you co-operate with us?" The man was obviously in some kind of commanding position. He had intricate metal studs on both collars. Ian looked around. The rest of the people were either in white lab coats or in the military type uniform. All had the John Titor insignia on their sleeves.

"Yes, I suppose so," said Ian. He was not sure where he was, and worse didn't know what year he was in. But it looked like he was in the future. His surroundings could almost be like the Collider lab he was so familiar with. The same but different, he thought.

"Who are you anyway?"

"Just call me Commander," replied the steely-faced figure. He then issued instructions for some food and drink to be brought. "After you've eaten we'll have a little chat." There was a hint of intimidation in this last sentence.

Ian tried talking to some of the other personnel standing around, but he was met with silence and even a glare from some of the lab coats. Must be technicians, he thought. They look a bit pissed off with me. Ian was trying to adjust to his new surroundings. The lack of any information was making his situation a bit chilling. His mind flashed back to Lucy and her pleas for him not to go. Bit late now, he thought.

One of the soldiers appeared with a tray of food and drinks. There was the familiar Coke-a-Cola sign on what was a strange looking container. There were sandwiches, which were duly unwrapped for him. He peeled back what seemed to be a cross between bread and crackers, revealing a compressed slice of something and four slices of square tomato. Genetic manipulating, he thought. He took a bite. The food was very bland at first, but as soon as he took a dink of Coke, his mouth burst with the flavour of smoked ham and vine ripened tomatoes. He took another bite. Bland again. He chewed for a while, still the bland taste. As soon as he took a drink from the Coke container, again his mouth filled with flavour. He tried just drinking the Coke alone. Just as Coke should taste! The container felt cold. Some kind of thermal receptacle he thought. He was just taking his last bite when the Commander suddenly appeared in front of him and signalled for one of the soldiers to take the tray away.

"Well, Ian. As I said you've caused us a major problem. Do you know where you are, or the date?"

Ian looked at him. He had eyes of steel. He had come across this type of man before. More of a fighting machine! No fear, no compassion, no remorse. Just get the job done.

"I presume that the machine we built has taken me, or should I say, brought me to 2038. Why is that such a problem?"

The Commander was now sitting opposite Ian. He tapped the table and an embedded touch screen appeared. He typed in some instructions. His steely gaze then focused on Ian.

"A friend is coming to meet you."

Ian was puzzled. Could it be Lucy, twenty years older? Or a geriatric Jim, he mused to himself.

Ian looked up as the figure appeared. Walking the distance from the lab doors was unmistakeably John Titor in his jump suit uniform. He was pushing some kind of trolley, but it had no wheels and seemed to be free of friction. He came to the commander's side. The now familiar IBM5100 was sitting on the trolley.

The Commander addressed Ian. "You messed with your super computer's memory. Do you know the damage you've done?"

"Well, first of all it was Mark, our IT specialist. He allowed our super computer to start to form Artificial Intelligence. It was, well, kind of arguing with us. So we had to erase the relative parts of its memory. There was no choice…"

"There's always a choice," snapped the Commander. "What you've done is give computers from that date a false time continuum memory."

Ian thought back to the issues Mark had had with his lap top date and time when it was plugged into Max.

"Now, John Titor here has to go back again to your lab to re-adjust your super computer. He also has to take this blasted IBM5100 back for re-adjustment, as it too was affected on John Titor's last trip."

Why doesn't he say John or Titor, why always use a first and last name, but now is not the time to ask, Ian reflected.

Ian looked around. His feet still firmly planted to the floor, but he was free to turn his body around. He could see his Time Machine and an instrument console." Is this a Particle Collider, is this how you travel in time?" He questioned the Commander, forgetting the precarious position he was in.

"I'm asking the questions," was the sharp reply. "John Titor is about to go back with this bloody box," he pointed to the IBM5100. "You will stay here until he returns safely."

"You can't keep me here." Ian suddenly realised how hazardous his situation was. Military personnel surrounded him and his feet were somehow glued to the floor, and now he was told that he would have to stay here until John Titor returned from another mission.

"You will stay here until John Titor comes back," the Commander glared at Ian. There was no room for argument.

"Can you at least release my feet so I can move around. I'm can't go anywhere and your armed guard here will ensure I don't do anything untoward."

"Such as?" sneered the Commander. He was now confident that Ian knew there was no escape. "Sit still and I'll release your feet for now." He again touched something on the table and the embedded screen appeared as if by magic. Ian could feel a lightening of his ankle. He moved his feet around in circular motions to get the circulation going again. "One touch of this screen and your feet will be locked no matter where you are."

So as long I have the boots on I can be locked to the floor, good to know, thought Ian. If I'm to get out of here I'll need all the odds to be with me.

The Commander summoned a couple of lab technicians. He gave what seemed clear instructions then turned to John Titor. This guy has earned his rank thought Ian. He begrudgingly had to give the guy credit for his continued command of the situation.

John Titor unzipped the front of his jump suit to reveal the flexi touch screen. He went to the command consol and plugged in a thin cable, which he had extended from the instrument on his chest. Ian was intrigued. They certainly had advanced the technology compared to, what now appeared to be his clumsy Time Machine.

Ian could hear a familiar rumble. It was the Collider starting up. It was different of course, but most of the changes just cosmetic. John Titor had unplugged the cable from the consol and was pushing the IBM5100 towards what Ian recognised was the start of the formation of a portal. As it reached the ultra violet spectrum, John Titor picked up the IBM and walked in. The now familiar shimmering was the precursor to his fading image.

Ian now reflected on his situation. Will I ever get back? My existence as I know it depends on John Titor having a successful mission. Would Mark and Lucy cope without him? He suddenly felt very alone.

# Chapter 20

There were no clocks on the walls, so Ian was having difficulty keeping track of time. Then he remembered the quartz clock in his Time Machine. He gradually manoeuvred to where he could see the clock. He was deliberately casual in his movements. These soldiers were armed and Ian was not exactly sure what orders they had, but it would be safe to assume that they were prepared to shoot him if necessary.

The Commander was busy at his table. Ian was fascinated with the embedded tablet he was using, but now was not the time for such things. He had to think, and think quickly. How would Mark and Lucy handle John Titor? He was sure that if it came to it Lucy would think outside the square and handle each situation as it occurred. The same could not be said for Mark. He didn't have the life experience, but then he certainly did have the logic that comes with IT learning.

Looking at the clock he noted the time. He would wait for how long, two hours? What then? The commander was not going to let him go easily. Even then, how would he get back to his time and Lucy without help of the lab technicians here?

The portal started to glow, a sure sign that something was happening. But it was only…. he didn't know, but certainly less than an hour. The now familiar ultra violet glowed as John Titor framed in the portal. But something was wrong. He did not have the IBM5100. Something was drastically wrong.

The wormhole stabilised and John Titor emerged. He didn't look up, but went straight to the Commander. His voice sounded angry, as he seemed to be relaying something. Suddenly, the Commander slapped John Titor so hard that he went flying across the floor. The Commander was bright red and had lost his composure. Even in this unpredicted situation Ian saw an advantage. The Commander had lost control, and for now Ian would have to take any opportunity he could.

"Who is Lucy?" the Commander was now leaning over Ian. His face red, blood vessels stood out on his forehead.

"She's in charge of our lab," Ian lied. He had no idea why he had done so, but he did have the advantage of now knowing what information the Commander had, or more to the point didn't have. "Why do you ask?"

"She kept our IBM5100 and sent John Titor back without your super computer being fully repaired. Do you know what that means?"

"Well I guess you have a problem," replied Ian calmly. Lucy had certainly kept her wits about her and returned John Titor back empty handed. He had remembered her saying how difficult it would be to get an IBM5100 as so few were made. Now it appeared John Titor had stolen at least one, probably two, if his calculations were correct.

"Send me back, I promise to return the IBM5100 and get Mark to finish the programming."

"I could have you shot on the spot," the Commander was still shouting. He was obviously not as in control as he would like to be. He was used to everyone following orders and getting results. This situation had him right on edge, while Ian felt a strange calm.

"Listen!" said Ian. "We're both on the same side as it were, only from different time continuums. Let me go back and I promise that I'll keep my word. I'll return the IBM and ensure Mark completes the super computer reprogramming. After all, my grandchildren will be coming to an uncertain future if the 2038 bug is not fixed. When computers start to run backwards, which will be very soon, all hell will break loose. It's in our mutual interest to let me go back."

"You're bloody joking! You'll stay right here until I work out what to do."

"Sergeant," he addressed one of the military men. "Guard him till I get back. The rest of you come with me. John Titor you've got some explaining to do on the video conference calls we're about to make to world leaders."

Ian sat down. He smiled at the sergeant who only gave him a frosty glare in return.

"I guess we just sit down and wait." Ian sat at the table with the embedded tablet. "I'll just put my head down and get some sleep."

"Do what you like," sneered the sergeant. Ian noticed that he was a bit more relaxed and in no way saw Ian as a threat.

Ian laid his head on the table. Very gradually he leant down to touch the boots. They were done up with some type of clasps. He slowly undid one, wondering if it was like Velcro and would make a noise when undone. He undid one, no sound. Great he thought. He slowly undid both boots without moving his head. Gradually he took his feet out. He sat up and stretched. The sergeant was looking bored. He had put his rifle type weapon down on the table. Ian noticed he still had a holstered sidearm. How quickly can he get it out, take the safety off and fire it, he wondered. Ian tried to engage the sergeant in conversation, but he wasn't interested. Ian figured he wasn't interested in much but just getting his pay every month, and following orders with no need to think.

Ian heard the doors at the end of the lab open. One of the techs was returning. Ian waited. It wasn't long before the soldier was in conversation with the tech. They were both betting men, it seemed. They were discussing the fight programmed for tonight. Not a lot changes, thought Ian.

He would have to wait for an opportunity. His patience paid off. The sergeant and tech were leaning over the computer consol laying bets for the fight.

Suddenly Ian stood up, grabbed the rifle and pointed it at the sergeant. "Keep your hands behind your heads, both of you." Ian approached and removed the side arm from the sergeant's holster. He was too fast. The safety wasn't on and it fired, right into the soldier's foot.

Without a blink Ian said, "The next one will be through your head, understand?" The sergeant was in extreme pain holding his foot, but managed to nod. Ian turned to the tech, who was now shaking.

"This is what's going to happen," Ian said with a newfound confidence. He turned to the sergeant. "Put the boots on."

"I can't he protested," blood was gushing from his foot. Must have hit a small artery, thought Ian. But he had no time for regret.

"Just put them on, if nothing else it will stem the bleeding."

"You!" He pointed the rifle at the tech. "Lock his boots to the floor. Don't tell me you don't know how." Fearing he was next for a bullet he didn't hesitate. He was a tech. No military training, fearing for his life, thought Ian.

Ian kept facing the sergeant, but had the tech buy the scruff off the neck.

"You're going to set my time continuum for the Collider and help me put my machine into the portal when it stabilises. Remember, I know all the co-ordinates, so if you try anything I'll shoot you in the foot. Do you have a preference which one?"

"Don't worry, I'll be precise," said the tech. "Please don't harm me. I have a wife and two children." There were tears in the techs eyes. Ian could see by the wet patch on his trouser front; he had already wet himself. Ian wondered at his newfound personal façade. He knew Lucy would be shocked, especially shooting someone in the foot. But it was an accident; he had only taken advantage of it, he convinced himself.

The sergeant was whimpering at the table as the tech helped Ian get the machine ready to load into the Collider. "Here, we'll put it on the trolley," said the tech. They manoeuvred the machine on, and then the tech pressed a button on the trolley handle. It started to elevate. He stopped when it was exactly at the right height.

"OK!" said Ian getting into his machine. He had checked the co-ordinates when the tech put them in. Ian was not sure on one point, so he questioned the tech, but he assured Ian it was correct. With a gun at his head Ian was quite confident there would be no mistake. The ultra violet spectrum hue was vivid and the mass seemed to be stabilised.

"Go!" commanded Ian.

He went through the same bumping then jackhammer feeling his body was going through just before he saw the familiar flash of white.

He gradually opened his eyes. He had been knocked unconscious at a football match once and the feeling of becoming conscious was the same just now. Where am I? He thought. He then looked up and saw Lucy. She had a terrified look on her face. Has the trip distorted my body? Am I a freak with stretched out facial features? he wondered. He was still confused. Lucy was shouting at him.

"Put it down. Ian! Put it down."

He looked down, then realised he was still holding the rifle!

# Chapter 21

Ian awoke to find Lucy sitting on his bed. Then he realised he was in her room and her bed. He was confused. What had happened, why was he lying here with Lucy's concerned eyes looking into his? It gradually came back to him; the return journey in the Time Machine, Lucy screaming at him, the rifle still in his hands.

"How long have I been sleeping?" he asked.

"About a day."

He felt a pang of guilt. How could he have slept for so long? He was not a lazy person by any means. He should have been up hours ago. He sat up and was about to jump out of bed, but his body was wracked with pain. It felt as if his whole being was bruised. He reluctantly lay back down again. He tried to gather his thoughts. Lucy was still holding his hand, as if to say, everything is OK, just take it easy.

"What happened?"

Lucy related the return of John Titor, and all the details of what had happened and how she had stopped Mark from finishing the re-programming. She told how she had managed to keep the IBM5100 and how she had sent him back empty handed. She said it was the only thing she could think of to do. She also said she had been terrified of losing him. She lay down on the bed and held him tight. She desperately wanted to hear his story, but thought she should wait until he was fully recovered.

But Ian didn't wait, and in turn related his story. The Commander. The special lock boots. How he had wrestled the gun from the sergeant. He refrained from mentioning shooting him in the foot, as he knew Lucy would not approve of the persona that had engulfed him. Apart from that he related all the interesting details; the food experience with the Coke drink, the travel suit of John Titor, the embedded tablet in the table, the problem they were having with the imminent 2038 computer bug and how Mark had messed with Max's memory and affected future time continuum apart from the already recognised 2038 bug.

"I don't know why my body is so stiff and racked with pain," Ian looked at Lucy. He was still feeling confused and hated being in this state of mind.

"John Titor explained that his Time Machine was a flexible tablet on his chest, but also the jump suit was part of his mode of time travel. It's possible that his suit absorbs the body jarring during the start and end of travel. He seemed quite composed, no sign of weakening of his joints."

"Makes sense," said Ian as he thought through Lucy's estimation of the technology. Ian was only too well aware how advanced life was in 2038.

After a while, Ian sensed that something was troubling Lucy. He was feeling a lot more coherent now, and wanted to get back to the lab.

"Something's wrong," he said looking directly into her eyes.

"Jim's back," she said. Her face told him that there was a major problem. "He wants to see all three of us as soon as you wake up. He's furious." She shrugged her shoulders as if to say he's never going to understand.

"OK. What time is it?"

"About ten!"

"In the morning?"

She nodded in the affirmative.

"Let's get something to eat, then we'll go to see him."
He was really too tired to face Jim, but felt that they should
get it over and done with.

"I'll get some sandwiches and Coke." She smiled for the
first time since his return. "Smoked Ham and vine ripened
tomato filling, with a can of Coke to wash it down." Her
sense of humour was infectious. He smiled and thought
how lucky he was to have her.

"Make an appointment to see Jim at one o'clock. Ask
Mark to come to your room now." He added the word
'please' as an afterthought.

Ian had the usual ravenous appetite that seemed to
accompany time travel, so he was glad that Lucy had
brought two packs of sandwiches and two Cokes.

Mark arrived as Ian was tucking into the last of the
second pack. He motioned Mark to sit down. He finished
chewing and downed the last of the Coke.

He looked at both of them. "I think that we should finish
the re-programming of Max and then send the terabyte hard
drive and the IBM5100 back. I'm thinking of the future of
mankind. If they don't fix the bug in 2038 and computers
run backwards, which they will, *Mad Max* movies will look
like a fairy tale. Food, water, and fuel will run out. Flights
will be grounded. Sewage plants will stop. Survival
instincts will kick in, and all hell will break loose. There
will be looting, rioting, even killing for a can of soup! The
only ones to survive will be the 'doomsday preppers', the
ones prepared for World War III, but they will eventually
turn on each other. In summary humankind will wipe it's
self out. I'm sure that in the analogues of time, man has
faced disasters on a mammoth scale, but we survived. But I
can't see us surviving this." They were both looking at Ian,
absorbing his words.

Lucy was the first to speak. "When you put it like that, I guess we have a duty to mankind to do as you say. But I dislike that John Titor intensely. I don't want to give him anything, and look how they treated you."

Ian sighed. "We have to look at the big picture, we have a duty. We can't take any of it personally. I've thought it through, we have to think of our children and grandchildren."

Lucy looked at him. Grandchildren, did he want children? They had never discussed such a personal topic. This put a whole new slant on her thinking.

"Yeah, I guess you're right. But remember the way they held you to ransom, should we just forget what they were prepared to do? They'd probably kill any of us if need be to get what they wanted." She was stubborn by nature and this was showing now, like never before.

Mark interceded. "Well for what it's worth, I agree with Ian. It was me who stuffed up with Max. I have to take some responsibility and make good as best I can."

Lucy nodded, reluctantly agreeing. "They shouldn't get away with it, but yes, I agree too."

"OK," said Ian. " Mark, finish the re-programming. Lucy can you help me start the Collider. We'll lift the machine with the IBM5100 back into the wormhole when it forms. We'll probably never see the machine again. Best to send it back unmanned." Ian thought of the sergeant and his wounded foot, he certainly wouldn't be welcome.

"We're not supposed to be using the Collider," Mark said sheepishly. "Jim has banned us from using it."

"Can you get access for enough time to do what we need to do?" Ian was back to himself, taking charge again.

"Yeah, I guess. But Jim said my job is on the line." Mark didn't know who to be more afraid of at this moment, Ian or Jim.

"Do it now!" Ian ordered. "Get us uninterrupted access for whatever time we need to complete what we've discussed and agreed."

Mark got busy on his laptop, which Ian noticed was plugged into Max.

"Does Max have to be involved?" asked Ian, knowing the answer before he asked. Mark looked up momentarily a red glow to his cheeks, embarrassed by the knowledge of all the trouble he had inadvertently caused.

"We'll have to go now, and we'll need to be quick," Mark said, moving to the lifts with his laptop under his arm.

They were now in the familiar Physics lab. Yellow 'DANGER' tape was fencing it off. The Time Machine was wrapped in plastic. Ian looked at Mark and Lucy, aghast at the sight.

"Jim's orders," Mark told him.

"Quick," said Ian, "help me get this tape and wrapping off." They all worked quickly to access the Time Machine and unravel it from its plastic bondage.

"Where's our trolley and slide?"

"Jim ordered all this wrapping of the machine and the removal of anything connected to it."

"Where's the IBM5100?"

"Down at the end of the lab. They're about to dismantle it."

"Just in time then," said Ian as he summoned them to give him a hand.

Ian started the Collider and they waited for the now familiar ultra violet wormhole to appear.

"We'll just have to load it manually," said Ian.

The machine was heavy, but they managed.

"Now the IBM," Ian ordered, and they loaded it.

Mark suddenly remembered the terabyte hard drive and placed it on top of the IBM box just in time.

The machine with its load faded as the shimmering finally stopped. They closed the Collider down.

"Time to see Jim," said Ian. He had a new found confidence. He was back to his cavalier self. The effects of time travel had apparently worn off.

They walked into Jim's office reception. Ian didn't wait, but just barged in to the main office. Jim closed his computer down, but not before they all could see the porn sight he had been ogling.

"Not disturbing you are we, Jim?" Jim was turning red, spluttering something about not just barging in when he was busy.

"I didn't know porn was part of your job description." Ian was now in control and Jim knew it.

"Look!" Jim was trying to get the upper hand but failing miserably. "What's all this time travel nonsense. Tying up lab and computer time! I could have you fired."

Ian was relaxed and totally in control.

"I don't work for you, I'm contracted to CERN. So perhaps you should check out my contract before making such threats. But we're here to tell you that we've finished with time travel. We have sent the machine to 2038 on a one-way trip. We loaded it with that old IBM computer you were about to dismantle. The balance of time and the future was at risk, but we've rectified all that so, I for one, am ready to start a new project."

"Me too!" Lucy offered.

"We will of course, in the fullness of time, submit to your office a complete written report on exactly what has transpired over the past few weeks. But first Lucy and I are taking a much-earned break. We'll let you get back to your porn." With that he stood up and they all walked out.

"You handled that really well!" Lucy's admiration was obvious.

Ian turned to Mark, "I hope you've learned something from everything that's happened."

Mark nodded. "What if Jim fires me? I'm not on a contract."

"Get Max to keep a record of his Internet searches and send a copy to him. Sign it best wishes Ian, Lucy, and Mark."

Lucy took Ian's arm as they walked to her room. Mark bid them farewell at the lifts. "Suppose we won't see you for a while," he said.

"No, we're off on a month's leave." Looking at Lucy, he said, "We have to consider the future for our children and grandchildren."

A feeling of warmth washed down Lucy's body. She had never felt this way before, but she wouldn't swap it for anything.

Printed in Great Britain
by Amazon.co.uk, Ltd.,
Marston Gate.